Jenny was the first one to tell me what happened.
"How can you look so calm? Haven't you heard?"

"Heard what?"

"Bunny Powers saw you in Pittsford with Doug on
Saturday and she's out there blabbing it to everyone."

When I heard that I hit the roof. "It's none of her
business who I date!"

"Sure, but if you want to keep any friends around here,
you better stay away from P. C. football players.
Besides," asked Jenny, "what about Alan? Does he
know?"

"I was going to tell him, but—oh, Jenny, what am I
going to do?"

"Well, Claire, there's only one thing you can
do . . ."

Caprice Romances from Tempo Books

A CAPRICE ROMANCE

Senior Blues
Francess Lin Lantz

TEMPO BOOKS, NEW YORK

SENIOR BLUES

A Tempo Book / published by arrangement with
the author

PRINTING HISTORY
Tempo Original / August 1984

ISBN: 0-441-75889-4

Tempo Books are published by The Berkley Publishing Group,
200 Madison Avenue, New York, New York 10016.
Tempo Books are registered in the United States Patent Office.
PRINTED IN THE UNITED STATES OF AMERICA

*To John
For all the driving, all the listening,
and all the love.*

Senior Blues

Chapter One

The Greyhound bus roared out of Boston, heading west across Massachusetts. I was sitting in a window seat with my nose pressed against the glass, watching the tall buildings whizz by. Gradually they were replaced by highway signs and billboards, and finally by green fields.

With a sigh, I leaned back in my seat and opened my magazine. Flipping past the fashion pages and the short stories, I turned to the quiz: "What Kind of Person Are You? Three Questions That Reveal More About You Than You Might Think!"

I'm a sucker for those personality quizzes. You know, the ones in *Seventeen* and *Cosmopolitan* with titles like "Are You Your Own Worst Enemy?" and "Test Your Romance IQ." They're silly, I guess, but somehow reassuring. I mean, it feels good to know I'm a "Personality Kid" (as I learned from taking "Do You Knock 'Em Dead or Leave 'Em Cold?") and that my Cuddle Quotient is 9½ out of 10.

Besides, some of those tests make a lot of sense. Like

1

the quiz I was reading in the bus, for example. It said that you can learn a lot about a person by asking three simple questions. One: Which do you like better—dogs or cats? Two: Which kind of ice cream do you prefer—vanilla or chocolate? And three: Where would you rather live—the city or the country?

Before I tell you what I learned from this quiz, I have to explain something about my family. On the day I was taking the bus home from Boston, my parents had been separated exactly three months. My mom was living in Boston, in a communal house she shared with four other people. In the daytime she worked in a vegetarian restaurant and at night she took courses at Northeastern University. I was living with my father in an old stone farmhouse in Miller's Creek, a dinky little town in the middle of nowhere.

Considering the three questions quiz, it was easy to see why Mom had left. She likes dogs, chocolate ice cream, and city living. My dad goes for cats, vanilla, and the great outdoors. As for me, although I look like my father (curly brown hair, blue eyes, long legs, and a short nose), talk like my father (too fast), and walk like my father (long, loping strides), our personalities are as different as vanilla ice cream with whipped cream and chocolate with hot fudge.

If it had been up to me, I would have moved to Boston with my mother. It's not that I don't love my father. I do. He's funny, easy going, and he doesn't make me clean up my room. But he's also a genuine, dyed-in-the-wool country boy. His idea of a good time is growing vegetables, fishing and hanging around the firehouse, shooting the breeze with his friends.

He doesn't mind that Miller's Creek has a population of less than five thousand, that there's no bookstore or record store, or that the five and ten sells clothes from 1959. In fact, he likes it. He says Miller's Creek is unspoiled and scenic. A slice of real Americana. I say it's dull, dull, dull.

As the bus followed the highway through rolling farmlands, I thought about the week I'd just spent in Boston with my mom. During the day we toured the city—shopping on Newbury Street, walking the Freedom Trail, eating in the Italian North End. In the evening we took her German shepherd, Mindy, to the park. At night we hung around with her roommates, eating popcorn and watching reruns of *Saturday Night Live*. Everything was great until I asked her why I had to go back to Miller's Creek.

"Oh, Claire, you don't want to stay here," she told me. "For one thing, there's no one to look after you. I'm out half the day and I take classes at night. Besides, the school system is lousy."

"Mom," I protested, "I'm seventeen. I don't need to be looked after."

"Miller's Creek is a nice place to grow up," she said. "You need a house, a yard, a group of close friends. Next year you'll be going to college and if you want to pick a city school, that's fine. Until then, stay with your father. He needs you."

"But Mom," I said softly, "what about you?"

Mom smiled and ran her hand over my hair. "I need to know you love me, and I hope you realize how much I love you. Right now, though, I really want to be alone. Can you understand that?"

"Sure," I said, trying to believe it. In the end, we

dropped the subject and went out for chocolate ice cream instead.

It was getting dark when the bus pulled into Miller's Creek. It had been a long trip and my neck was stiff from sleeping with my head against the window. I looked out at Main Street—Hafner's Drug Store, the firehouse, the Main Street Tavern—everything looked the same as it always had.

And there was my dad, waiting for me with his hands on his hips and a crooked smile on his face. He looked glad to see me, and suddenly I felt kind of happy to see him, too. I closed my magazine, shoved it into my shoulder bag, and hurried off the bus to be hugged.

The next week marked the beginning of my senior year at the Mill—Miller's Township Regional High School. The school is tiny—only two hundred students from three towns—and of course everybody knows everybody else. In fact, most of the kids have gone to school together since kindergarten. In a way it's nice—kind of like one big happy family. In another sense, though, the place can really get on your nerves.

For one thing, everybody gets typecast. People form an impression of who you are (usually based on something you did in grade school) and you're pegged for life. You can't change because no one will let you. I, for example, am known as a nice kid, talkative, a little goofy, and reasonably smart. It wouldn't matter if I flunked all my courses, took a vow of silence, or won the Nobel Prize. Everybody would still treat me like the same old Claire Mason they'd always known—a nice kid, talkative, a little goofy, and— Well, you get the idea.

I also have another claim to fame. People are still laughing about the time I threw up in the middle of the third grade production of *Cinderella*. Like I said, pegged for life.

The other problem with a small school is that there's only a limited number of people you can date. News travels fast around the Mill, so naturally you don't want to go out with someone unattractive, or unpopular, or from the wrong clique. That leaves about ten guys to choose from, and usually you know them all so well it's about as exciting as dating your big brother.

The first day of school was hectic, as always. I walked into the lobby and joined the crowd of kids who stood around talking and laughing. People waved to me and a dozen friends stopped to ask me about my summer or tell me the latest gossip.

I giggled and gossiped like everyone else, but my heart wasn't in it. I was thinking about being in Boston with my mom. I loved the crowded streets, the busy stores, the sidewalk cafes. All they have in Miller's Creek are pizza shops, fast-food chains and The Merry Meal—a family restaurant that specializes in tuna casserole.

I looked around the crowded high school lobby and sighed. Everybody looked the same. They wore the same clothes, the same hairstyles, the same bland expressions. Not like the kids I'd seen in Boston. They came in all sizes, shapes, and colors, and they dressed in every style imaginable, from preppie to punk.

How I wished I was going to high school with them! Not only would there be dozens of new people to meet, but I'd be a new person, too. No one would remember me as Queasy Claire, the girl who threw up all over Prince

Charming. I'd be Claire Mason—beautiful, mysterious, desirable. "Who's that new girl?" the guys would ask each other. "She's not like anybody else around here. She's special."

"Guess who?" Someone had put his hands over my eyes and for a moment I thought it was part of my daydream. Maybe when I opened my eyes I really would be in Boston. I'd lift the hands off my face, turn around, and find . . .

Alan Wallant. "Were you surprised?" he asked, leaning down and kissing the tip of my nose.

Alan has been my boyfriend for two years. He's a tall, lanky guy with straight blond hair, gray eyes, and an easy grin. He's the president of the student council and, incidentally, the Prince Charming I threw up on in third grade.

"Yes," I told him. "You had me completely baffled. I was expecting Rin Tin Tin."

"Woof!" said Alan. "Arf, arf!" He grabbed me and enthusiastically licked my cheek.

"Yuck!" I cried, laughing and pulling away. "Down, boy, down!"

Alan grinned. "How was your trip to Boston? How's your mom?"

"Great," I said. "Boston is so exciting. It's a real letdown to be back."

Alan looked a little hurt, and I was sorry I'd said anything. It wasn't really Alan I was bored with, just Miller's Creek. Alan, I reminded myself, was a wonderful guy—sweet, easygoing, loyal, predictable . . . Well, maybe I *was* just a tiny bit bored with him. After all, we'd known each other practically all our lives and we'd been dating steadily for two years. I liked Alan, but sometimes

6

he seemed more like an old pal than a boyfriend.

My thoughts left me feeling guilty and disloyal, and I quickly changed the subject. "You know, I read an article yesterday that said you could tell a lot about a person by asking three basic questions."

"Oh, yeah?" Alan knew all about my fanatical devotion to magazine quizzes. He thought I was a little crazy, but he always humored me when I was on my latest personality kick.

"Now listen," I said. "Which do you like better—dogs or cats?"

"I prefer slugs."

"Alan, come on!" I gave him a punch on the arm.

He pretended to cower. "Okay, okay, just don't get violent. I like dogs."

"Me, too. That means you're outgoing, lovable, and sincere. Now how about ice cream? Do you like chocolate or vanilla?"

"You know I always eat butter almond." I raised a threatening fist. "Well, chocolate," he conceded.

"Me, too. That's a sign of a strong, directed personality. Now, one more. Where would you rather live—the city or the country?"

"That one's easy. I like the country. Green fields, lakes, farmland." Alan hooked his thumbs in imaginary overalls. "No, ma'am, that wild city livin' just ain't for me."

Well, I thought halfheartedly, two out of three isn't bad. Anyway, I already knew Alan was a country boy. His dream was to go to medical school and then set up practice in Miller's Creek as an old-fashioned GP, housecalls and all.

"Well," asked Alan, "what does that say about me? Come on, Ms. Psychologist, I can take it."

It means you're boring, I wanted to say. Boring as Main Street on a Sunday afternoon. Instead I said, "It means you're relaxed, inner-directed, and as American as apple pie."

"That's me." Alan laughed. "Okay, I took the test. Now what do I win?"

"You win the right to walk me to homeroom," I told him. "Lucky guy."

Alan laughed and took my hand. "That Boston air must have done something to your brain. You're nuttier than ever." I put on a fake pout and Alan added quickly, "But I like it, I like it. Come on, world traveler. Let's go."

I didn't see Alan again until the fifth-period student council meeting. It was the first meeting of the year, and everybody was anxious to hear what Alan had to say. During his campaign last year, he'd promised to improve student/teacher communication, institute a senior class trip, and expand extracurricular activities. Now he had to make good his promises with some concrete plans.

I knew Alan had met with the principal, Mr. Bower, while I was in Boston, but I had no idea what they'd discussed. All I knew was that Bower was a pretty conservative guy and Alan had been worried the administration would veto all his plans.

I was the student council representative from my homeroom. I took a seat with the other reps and looked around for Alan. He was sitting at a long table at the front of the auditorium talking to Suzie Baynor, the vice-president, and Jon Van Doren, the treasurer. Alan saw me and smiled.

"Hey, Claire." I turned and saw Rob Thayer leaning across the aisle. "Did Alan set up a senior trip?"

"Yeah, to Hawaii?" asked someone else in the row.

"I don't know," I admitted. "He met with Mr. Bower, but I was in Boston last week. I don't know any more than you do."

"Come on," urged Rob. "You're supposed to be our inside line to the president."

"Yeah," agreed someone else. "Our secret source. Our leak."

Everyone laughed until Alan rapped his gavel on the table and said, "The first meeting of the Miller's Township Regional High School student council will now come to order."

I looked up at Alan. From the way he rubbed his palms against the sides of his jeans, I could tell he was nervous. He cleared his throat and ran a hand through his hair. A few stray hairs stuck out on the sides and I longed to reach up and pat them down.

Despite Alan's slightly disheveled appearance, I had to admit he looked good. His gray eyes were deep and serious and his light-blue Izod shirt fit tightly across his chest and over his flat stomach. I caught his eyes and stuck out my tongue to make him grin.

"As promised," he began, a little more confident now, "I met with Mr. Bower to discuss my ideas for the new school year." He paused. "Well, there's some good news and some bad news." Everybody groaned. "First, the bad news. So far, I haven't been able to get permission for a senior class trip. Mr. Bower feels it's too expensive and requires too much organization." More groans. "But we won't give up that easily. I'd like to set up a committee to look into the idea. You know, places we could go, costs,

9

number of chaperones required, all of that.''

Someone made a motion to start the committee and it was quickly passed. Alan appointed Heather Baum as its chairman.

''Now the good news. Mr. Bower agreed to a student/ faculty committee that would meet twice a month to discuss problems and hopefully even have the power to abolish and create school rules.''

Everyone cheered and Alan added, ''Also, Mr. Bower and I discussed expanding the school's extracurricular activities. For example, a computer club, a new cheerleading squad for males as well as females, and something really special—an exchange program with other schools.''

Huh? Alan had never mentioned that he was interested in an exchange program. I leaned forward and listened closely.

''We've even set up our first one-day exchange. It's with Pittsford Central. Anyone interested in going should see me after this meeting.''

Pittsford Central? Pittsford is about twenty miles from Miller's Creek and it's a real city. Nothing like Boston, of course, but it's the closest thing to an urban center we've got. It's got department stores, restaurants, parks, and little ethnic neighborhoods. When my mom was around we used to do all our clothes shopping there, and every Christmas when I was little my folks took me there to sit on Santa Claus's lap.

Since Mom left, however, I hadn't been to Pittsford once. ''There's no place to park,'' my dad would say whenever I suggested we drive there. ''Why can't you just go over to the mall if you need some clothes?''

"But Dad," I'd tell him, "it's not the same. Pittsford is more exciting."

"Also more crowded, more expensive, and more dangerous." To hear my dad talk, you'd think Pittsford was a regular Sin City—bigger, dirtier, and scarier than the Big Apple itself.

The rest of the student council meeting was devoted to a discussion of Homecoming and the prom. I listened well enough to report back to my homeroom, but my mind was really on the new exchange program. Going to P. C. would be a great way to get out of Miller's Creek, even if it was only for one day.

Who knows, I told myself, maybe I could make some new friends, even meet some boys. Not that I wanted to go out with anyone except Alan, of course, but it would be nice to at least see some new faces. And if they were handsome male faces, attached to tall, well-built male bodies . . . well, so much the better.

Right then and there I decided I was going on that exchange. When the student council meeting ended, I jumped up and made my way toward Alan. "Pittsford Central," I whispered, "here I come!"

Chapter Two

It turned out I wasn't the only one trying to talk to Alan.
Other people wanted to ask him about the exchange program, too, but not for the same reason.

"What's the idea of an exchange with Pittsford Central?" I heard someone saying. "We don't want those
kids at our school."

"Yeah," agreed someone else. "They'll probably just
sneak into football practice and try to steal our plays."

"That's an idea!" exclaimed Jon Van Doren. "Maybe
we can get a chance to steal theirs."

I stopped, surprised and confused. What was the big
deal? I wondered. What was all this talk about stealing
football plays? And what did it have to do with an exchange between Pittsford Central and the Mill?

Then I remembered. I had been so excited about the
possibility of spending the day in Pittsford that I had
totally forgotten about football. You see, at Miller's
Township Regional High School, everybody talks, eats,

drinks, and breathes football. That's because, despite our size, we have one of the best high school football teams in the area. Last year we lost only one game all season and we even went on to the state championships. The only school that beat us was our number-one rival. Yes, you guessed it—Pittsford Central.

I don't know a lot about football. I understand the basic rules and I can throw around a few terms like first down, handoff, and punt, but I'm hardly what you'd call a big fan. Still, like everyone else at the Mill, I go to the games and make myself hoarse rooting for our team. After all, there's nothing else to do on a Saturday afternoon in Miller's Creek. And even if I don't love football, I do enjoy sitting around with my friends, eating popcorn and hot dogs, and cheering the home team on to victory.

But that had nothing to do with a one-day exchange. Just because P. C. had beaten us in football last year, that was no reason to act like the whole school had the plague or something. Obviously Alan agreed with me.

"Now listen," he was saying, "the whole point of this exchange program is to learn about other schools, other towns, and other kids. Just because P. C. is our rival on the football field doesn't mean they're our enemies in the classroom as well. Maybe if we do enough of these exchanges, people will understand that and all this football vandalism will stop."

I had pretty much forgotten about last year's craziness, but when Alan mentioned football vandalism, it all came back to me. The whole thing had started when some kids from the Mill drove over to Pittsford and sprayed black and gold paint (our school colors) all over the entrance to the P. C. football stadium. No one was caught, but everybody suspected the culprits were Barry Fitch and Matt Rosselli, two of the wildest kids in the marching band.

Pittsford Central retaliated by painting SULTANS STINK, RAVENS RULE on the front door of the Mill in two-foot-high red letters. Again, no one was caught. Before the Mill could strike again, the two schools met on the football field. A fistfight broke out in the stands and two players were thrown out of the game for arguing before P. C. finally won, 21–13.

Naturally the Mill swore revenge and that night the P. C. coach found the tires of his car slashed. The whole thing ended when the police warned both schools that any further vandalism would be punished by canceling the Homecoming dance, and if necessary, the prom.

Alan, I'm proud to say, was the first student council presidential candidate to speak out against the vandalism. Thanks to his articles in the school newspaper (and the threats by the police) the craziness had stopped before anything really serious happened.

The vandalism might have ended, but considering the response Alan was getting to his exchange program, the Mill/P. C. antagonism was still going strong. "You're not going to find anyone who'll want to spend the day at Pittsford Central," argued Heather Baum.

"I sure wouldn't go," Suzie Baynor agreed. "They're nuts over there. They'd probably beat me up."

That was it. I couldn't keep quiet any longer. Disgusted, I stepped forward and said loudly, "I'll go!" Everyone turned and looked at me as I walked over and stood next to Alan. "Why not?" I challenged. "It sounds like fun."

"All right!" Alan told the crowd. "Here's one brave

15

person who dares to enter enemy territory. Maybe it's because she's been all the way to Boston and returned to tell the tale.''

I laughed. ''Right. And can you believe it? The people there look just like us. Two eyes, one nose, one mouth. I'll let you know if the P. C. kids are the same.''

''Okay, okay,'' Jon Van Doren conceded. ''We get the point.''

Just then the bell rang and everyone hurried to find their books and leave. As the auditorium emptied, Alan put his arm around me and gave me a kiss. ''Thanks,'' he said. ''I knew I could count on you.''

I smiled but I didn't answer. I guess I was feeling a little guilty. Alan thought I wanted to go on the exchange to further friendship and understanding between the two schools. He didn't know my real motive was to get out of Miller's Creek and into the city for the day. Guiltily, I recalled my dream of meeting some good-looking boys. And meanwhile, here was Alan, encouraging me to go on the exchange. If he only knew!

''And when you come back,'' he added, ''you can write an article for the school paper. You know, let everyone know the kids at P. C. are just like us.''

''An article?'' I moaned. ''Oh, come on, Alan. You know I hate to write papers. Besides, Mrs. Radnor is the adviser of the newspaper and I can't stand her. She gave me a C in English last year.''

I had a few more things to say about Mrs. Radnor, but I stopped when I saw the expression on Alan's face. He looked so earnest, so concerned, so sincere that I could have kicked myself for wanting to meet anyone new. Alan was a great person, even if he was a small town guy, and

16

he was enough for any girl. Before he could say anything, I kissed his cheek and said, "Don't worry, Alan. I'll write a great article for the paper. I promise."

In the end, it was Jenny Pilsner who went on the exchange with me. Jenny is probably my best friend in Miller's Creek, and her boyfriend, Ben Miles, is a good friend of Alan's. Jenny shares my feelings about football, and, although she likes Miller's Creek, she shares my enthusiasm for Pittsford as well. Furthermore she's not the type to get carried away by interschool rivalry. All in all, I couldn't think of anyone I'd rather have with me on the exchange.

Jenny and I had big plans for our day in Pittsford. After school ended, we would stay in the city, go shopping, and eat at one of the little restaurants on Broad Street. Despite my dad's feelings about Pittsford, he didn't argue. I think he realized that if I went to the city with Jenny, I would stop bugging *him* to take me—at least for a while.

The morning of the exchange, Dad made me blueberry pancakes and then went through his list of dos and don'ts. "Stay on the main streets, Claire," he told me. "Don't talk to anyone. And be home by dark."

"Dad," I moaned, "it's only Pittsford. Boston is much bigger."

"I know, but you were with your mother there. This is Jenny, and if I remember correctly, you two have a habit of getting into mischief together. Remember that time you decided to walk across Lake Pawtaug?"

"Oh, Dad," I protested, "that was three years ago!"

My father chuckled and sipped his coffee. "We had to take a boat out to pick you up." He shook his head. "I still can't believe you thought that lake was only three feet deep the whole way across.''

I giggled with embarrassment. "Come on, Dad," I told him. "We were just kids.''

The sound of Jenny's car turning into the driveway saved me from any more of my father's embarrassing reminiscences. Gulping down the last of my juice, I gave him a kiss and grabbed my jacket.

"I'll be out in the truck all day," he told me. "But call the office if you need me. They'll know where I am.''

My father is the building inspector of Miller's Township and I can't imagine a more perfect job for him. He gets to drive around the countryside, talking to people, inspecting new construction, and giving out permits. After ten years on the job, he knows every road, every house, and every person in the township. It sounds incredibly boring to me, but it's my father's idea of heaven.

Out in the driveway I found Jenny waiting in her family's brand-new orange Mustang. Despite the cool weather, she had the T-roof open. The radio was blasting the latest song by Duran Duran.

"Hi," I said, hopping in beside her. "Ready for our excursion behind enemy lines?''

"You bet. I've got the car outfitted with machine guns and a smoke screen. If that doesn't work, I'll release the ejector seat and leave you behind as a hostage.''

"Thanks a lot!" I put on my seat belt as Jenny backed out of the driveway and took off down Green Hill Lane. I noticed that, like me, she had spent some time on her appearance today. Her jeans were skintight and faded to perfection, and her blue-striped blouse and matching scarf had obviously been purchased in a Pittsford boutique. I

18

was wearing clothes I'd bought in Boston—black jeans that ended midcalf and a pink ruffled blouse with buttons up the side.

After a few minutes, we left Miller's Creek and turned onto Route 210. It still looked like a country road but it was smoother and faster and Jenny shifted the car into fourth. Pittsford was about forty-five minutes away, but at the rate Jenny was driving, I figured it would take us less than half an hour.

After a couple of minutes, Jenny turned down the radio. "Tell the truth, Claire," she said. "Do you think the kids at P. C. will give us a hard time?"

"I don't know. I doubt it. What can they do? Spray paint 'Ravens rule' on our foreheads?"

Jenny laughed. "You know, there are some good-looking guys in that school. Did you ever see the football team without their helmets? Real hunks!"

I nodded, wondering if Jenny's mind was working the same as mine. Maybe she was getting a little bored with Ben and hoping to meet someone new at Pittsford Central. But, I reminded myself, that wasn't the point of the exchange. The idea was to promote understanding, not romance. Besides, I wasn't looking for a boyfriend. I already had Alan.

As we approached Pittsford, the countryside turned to suburbs and then finally gave way to apartment houses and stores. I read the directions off the mimeographed sheet Alan had given us and in a few minutes we were turning into the parking lot of Pittsford Central.

The school is in the middle of town, next to the public library and city hall and across from a park. At first glance, the building looks a lot like a bigger version of the

19

Mill—a brick box with huge windows and an American flag over the door.

When we walked inside, however, the similarity ended. P. C. had been completely renovated and modernized. The floors were gleaming black linoleum and the windows were single panes of tinted glass. Lockers were either yellow, red, or blue and the classroom doors were green. Unlike the Mill, which looks as worn and familiar as last year's notebook, Pittsford Central was colorful, stylish, and new.

"Wow!" exclaimed Jenny. "Is this school gorgeous or what?"

"Really!" I took a few steps into the lobby and stopped. A few dozen kids were coming down the hall, walking in groups of two or three. Suddenly I felt extremely nervous. What if they could tell we were outsiders? Would they realize we were from the Mill and try to hassle us? I glanced at Jenny. She had stopped, too, and was staring uncomfortably at the floor.

But our fears were groundless. The kids walked by without giving us a glance and I allowed myself to relax. Jenny giggled nervously. "Well, I guess we passed the first test," she said.

I nodded. "Come on. We're supposed to check in at the office."

The secretary, it turned out, was expecting us. "We have two students who have volunteered to show you around today. Have a seat and I'll page them." She disappeared into another room and a moment later we heard her voice over the P.A. system. "Sarah Filmore and Doug Landsberg, report to the office please. Sarah Filmore and Doug Landsberg."

Hmm, one girl and one boy. I knew I wasn't supposed to care, but I couldn't help wondering what Doug Landsberg was like. Was he handsome? Was he nice? And most important, would he be Jenny's guide or mine? I glanced over at Jenny. She was looking eagerly toward the door and I was pretty sure she was wondering the same thing.

The next person to walk through the office door was a boy, and the first thing that flashed through my mind was, Oh, let him be my guide! He was tall and muscular with broad shoulders and a slender waist. His hair was dark and short, but still thick and wavy, and his face was rugged with deep-brown eyes, a firm mouth, and a cleft chin. He was wearing jeans and a Pittsford Central football jersey and—miracle of miracles—he was smiling right at me!

"Hi," he said, walking over to Jenny and me. "I'm Doug Landsberg."

Before either of us could respond, a small, cute redhead came through the door and joined him. "Hi. I'm Sarah. Are you the kids from the Mill?"

We introduced ourselves and Sarah said, "Do either of you girls play an instrument?"

"Uh, yes," answered Jenny. "I play the flute."

"Great. Then why don't you come with me? I'm in the orchestra and we have rehearsal today. You can probably even borrow a flute and join in."

Jenny's face fell and I could tell she wished she'd kept her mouth shut. Obviously, she wanted to spend the day hanging out with Doug, not talking music with perky little Sarah Filmore. For a moment I hesitated. I felt sorry for Jenny, but what could I do? I don't play an instrument and I couldn't think of any other reason—real or imaginary—

21

for spending the day with Sarah. Besides, Doug was looking at me, and the twinkle in his eyes made my knees feel weak.

"Well," he said suavely, "I guess that leaves you and me."

The intimate tone of his voice made my heart do a backward flip. "Right," I repeated foolishly. "You and me."

He smiled easily. "Well then, what are we waiting for?" Without a word to Jenny or Sarah, Doug put his hand against my back and guided me out the door.

Chapter Three

~~~~~~~~~~~~~~~~

"Well," said Doug as we walked down the hall, "so you're from the Mill." Suddenly he stopped, reached for my ear, and in one quick motion ran his fingers behind the lobe.

"Hey!" I cried, jumping back in alarm. "What's the big idea?"

Doug laughed. "Just checking to see if you have hay behind your ears."

I giggled and punched his arm. "Come on, no country bumpkin jokes. Pittsford isn't exactly New York City, you know."

"Okay, truce," he agreed. Doug smiled and the corners of his eyes crinkled up. "Let's be friends."

I looked at Doug and nodded. For some reason, I felt very excited. My heart was beating double time and I couldn't think of anything to say. All I could do was stare at Doug and marvel at how good-looking he was. His broad shoulders . . . his relaxed way of walking, with his arms swinging loosely at his sides . . . his dark eyes . . . the deep cleft in his chin . . .

"Here's my homeroom," he said, stopping by one of the green doors. "You may get a little flak from the kids today, but don't let it bother you." He raised his fists and spoke in a tough Sylvester Stallone voice. "I'll protect ya, kiddo. Come on."

As we walked into the classroom all eyes turned our way. I followed Doug to the back of the room and took a seat next to him. The teacher—an overweight middle-aged woman—was taking attendance. When she finished she said, "Class, we have a visitor with us today." She looked at me. "Would you like to come up and tell us a bit about your school?"

No, I wanted to say. Not at all. But I couldn't see that I had any choice. I was supposed to be an ambassador from the Mill. I couldn't just spend the whole day hiding behind Doug.

Slowly, I stood up and walked to the front of the class. I looked out at the sea of faces and said, "Hi. My name is Claire Mason. I live in Miller's Creek and go to Miller's Township Regional High School. We call it the Mill."

"Or the Mule," someone muttered. Everyone laughed.

"Too bad they can't kick like mules," someone else added. "They couldn't even get their field goal up in the air."

That was a reference to last year's game. Two of our field goals had been blocked by P. C. I forced myself to smile. "What can I say? You beat us."

"We will this year, too," said a girl in the back row.

This was getting very uncomfortable. I looked around for the teacher, but she was at the door, talking to someone out in the hall. "Hey," I began, "I'm not here to talk about football—"

"How about slashed tires?" asked a tough-looking kid in a leather jacket. "Are you here to talk about that?"

I could feel myself starting to sweat. This was turning into a really bad scene. "Come on," I muttered, "I—"

"Come on," squealed the tough kid, parodying my voice. "Be nice!" The class laughed. I looked back at Doug. He was laughing, too. Some protection! I thought to myself. Thanks a lot, Doug.

Then suddenly I had an inspiration. If I just made a joke out of the whole thing, maybe everyone would relax a little. "Well," I said quickly, "I'd just like to assure everyone that Miller's Township does have electricity and running water." A few giggles. "Our principal export is spray paint," I added, "and our football team is famous for kicking the ball into the arms of the opposing team." The class laughed.

Before I could say anything else, the teacher came back in and closed the door. Smiling sweetly, I sat down and glanced at Doug. He grinned back. "Way to go," he said.

After that the teacher read the announcements and a few minutes later the bell rang. The class left without giving me another look. "Come on," said Doug. "My first class is U.S. history." He took my elbow and moved me toward the door.

"Wow," I said as we walked down the hall. "Is the whole day going to be like that?"

He chuckled. "Don't let them bother you. They're just fooling around."

I didn't think Doug was taking things seriously enough. All this animosity between P. C. and the Mill was ridiculous. If things continued like this, I was pretty sure there was going to be a lot more vandalism this year, and maybe even some more fights. But when Doug smiled at me, I forgot about all that. He still had his hand on my elbow and I found myself wishing he would put his arm around my waist. It felt good to be near him.

"So," he asked, "what do you kids in Miller's Township do for kicks?"

"Well, it's pretty boring," I said. "We go to school dances or parties or the drive-in. In the summer we drive up to the lake. How about you?"

"I mostly cruise around the city," he said. "There are some good restaurants and a disco out on the highway."

I didn't want to admit it, but I had never been to a disco in my life. There weren't any around Miller's Creek and the only club I knew of—Buddy's in Pawtaug—served liquor and was for adults only. "Sounds great," I said. "I just got back from Boston and there was a lot of good nightlife there."

"You like the city?" he asked.

"Oh, yes. I love it."

He smiled and said, "Maybe some night you'd like to check out Pittsford with me."

Before I could answer three guys came up to Doug. They were all well built and athletic-looking like him. "Hey, Landsberg! What's happening?"

"Not much, guys." He nodded at me. "This is Claire from Miller's Creek."

"Well, what do you think of P. C. so far?" asked one of them, a black guy with muscles that outclassed even Doug's.

"I like it," I said. I pointed at the multicolored lockers.

"Great building."

"That's to wake us up in the morning." Doug chuckled. "But it doesn't work." He dropped his head on my shoulder and let out a noisy snore.

The guys laughed and moved off down the hall as Doug and I continued in the other direction. Nothing more was said about his suggestion that we explore Pittsford together and I wondered if maybe I'd imagined it. After all, Doug barely knew me. Why would he be asking me out? Anyway, he was so good-looking I was sure he had a girlfriend already. And come to think of it, I had a boyfriend, too. Feeling guilty, I realized I had been so charmed by Doug's good looks I'd practically forgotten about Alan. Promising to keep my mind on Alan, I followed Doug into his U.S. history class.

The morning went quickly as I sat in on Doug's history, English, and trig classes. In every class I had to get up and give a little talk about the Mill. Some kids acted bored and some looked disgusted, but most seemed pretty receptive. The trick, I now realized, was to make jokes, talk fast, and stay close to the teacher at all times. Like my fellow students at the Mill, the kids at P. C. liked to act smart and make wisecracks, but it didn't mean much. Sure, there were a few students at P. C. who really hated the Mill (and vice versa), but mostly it was just talk—acting tough and fooling around.

Through it all, I stayed close to Doug. He wasn't all that talkative—at least, not like Alan, who was one of the most articulate people I knew—but he was friendly, attentive, and funny. He didn't seem to take things too seriously and his easygoing manner and masculine good looks really appealed to me.

I kept waiting for Doug to tell me he had a girlfriend, but he didn't say a word about girls. Mostly he talked about Pittsford and all the places he and his friends went, like Gino's Italian Villa, the Golden Dragon Restaurant, and the Flames, Pittsford's disco. He also told me about the public pool down by the river, where you could sneak in and go swimming after dark, and the water tower you could climb to get a view of the whole city. It all sounded pretty scary to me, but at the same time Doug's adventures fascinated and thrilled me. I was already bored to tears with Miller's Creek and listening to Doug just reinforced my feelings. Pittsford was an exciting place!

When the bell rang for lunch, Doug took me to the cafeteria. The place was huge compared to our little lunchroom at the Mill, and the food was much more interesting. Doug steered me away from the hot lunches and led me toward the sandwiches.

"Get something small and we can carry it onto the roof," he said.

"The roof?" I repeated, but Doug only smiled mysteriously.

"Follow me," he said.

Armed with a sandwich and a can of soda, I followed Doug out of the cafeteria. In the hall, he looked around and then hurried me out the side door. The morning clouds had dispersed and it was turning into a beautiful fall day. It felt great to be outside, but I had a sneaking suspicion we weren't supposed to be here. No other students were in sight.

"Doug," I began, "are you sure—"

"Shhh," he answered. "Follow me."

Not knowing what else to do, I followed Doug around

to the back of the school. A metal ladder was attached to the side of the building, extending from the roof to about eight feet above the ground. Doug stopped in front of it and took my sandwich and soda out of my hands. "You climb up first," he said. "I'll be right behind you."

I looked up the ladder and then back at Doug. "Are you kidding?" I asked incredulously.

He smiled. "Of course not. Go on. It's an easy climb, and wait until you see the view. This is the best place to eat lunch in the whole city."

"But Doug," I protested, "I can't believe we're allowed to go up there."

"Well, let's put it this way," he said smoothly. "No one ever told me I couldn't." He paused and looked at me closely. "What's wrong? Are you scared?"

Well, of course I was scared, but I didn't want to tell Doug that. All morning he'd been telling me about the things he and his friends liked to do around town, and I'd been nodding and smiling and saying, "Great, great." Now he was offering me a chance to join in, and all I could think of was what would happen if the principal caught us or a strong wind knocked us down, or both.

Relax, Claire, I told myself. It's no big deal. Just climb up the ladder. Admittedly, I didn't know Doug very well, but I liked him and I just couldn't believe he would do anything to get us into trouble. Besides, I *wanted* to eat lunch on the roof. It sounded fun, daring, and maybe a little romantic, too.

"Okay," I said finally. "Give me a boost."

"Go for it!" Doug grabbed my waist and effortlessly lifted me until I could reach the ladder. I held on tight, got my feet firmly on the bottom rung, and then started to climb. I didn't look down but I could hear Doug behind me, the soda cans clanging softly against the ladder as he moved.

When I reached the top of the ladder I scrambled onto the flat, gravel-covered roof and looked around. City hall blocked the view in one direction, but the other three sides were clear. I could see over the rooftops in two directions and across the park in the third. The wind was cool and the sun was warm—a perfect combination. It felt great.

Doug appeared a second later. "Well," he asked, "what do you think?"

"I love it!"

Doug grinned at me. "I knew you would." Sitting down beside a chimney, he pulled the sandwiches and sodas out of his shirt. "Whew! These cans were freezing my stomach!"

I sat down beside him and we started to eat. Sipping my soda, I looked at Doug. His thick dark hair was being ruffled by the wind and his football jersey was flapping loosely against his broad chest. His arms were deeply tanned and his nose was peeling. He looked so handsome that I could hardly believe it. Here I was, sitting beside him on the roof of Pittsford Central. The danger, the knowledge that we weren't really supposed to be there, and the sight of Doug sitting only inches away gave me a heady feeling. For the first time since I'd returned from Boston, I felt terrific!

While we ate, Doug pointed out some of the things we could see around us. "I live over there," he said, pointing beyond the park. "Near that church. And see that field over there? That's where I played Pop Warner football. And look at that big tree at the edge of the park. That's a great tree to climb."

"Someday you should come to Miller's Creek," I told him. "Then I could show you around."

"Sure," he replied with twinkle in his eye. "That should take about five minutes and then we can drive back into town."

I laughed, but actually Doug's teasing had gone in one ear and out the other. What I was really interested in were the words "and then we can drive back into town." Did he mean together? As in a date?

Before I could pursue the idea, the bell rang. We could barely hear it on the roof, but Doug was immediately alert. "Come on," he said. "If we're late to class, somebody might come looking for us."

The idea of going down the ladder filled me with dread, but Doug was in such a hurry to get out of there that I forced myself to move. I made a point of not looking down and before I had time to get really nervous, I was at the bottom. It was only a short hop to the ground and then Doug took my hand and led me back around the building. He was so busy peering through the door to make sure no teachers were coming that he barely noticed I was there. I, on the other hand, wasn't aware of anything except Doug's hand firmly wrapped around mine.

We made it to chemistry just in time and after that we went to study hall and gym. Doug was in the same gym class as Sarah, so while the gym teacher led the class through a regimen of boring exercises, Jenny and I sat in the bleachers and talked.

"Well," I asked, "how's it going?"

"Okay," replied Jenny. "Sarah's kind of a Goody Two-Shoes, but she's all right. A few people have told me to go back to the farm, but no one has threatened me with violence."

"Same here, but someone in homeroom brought up the slashed tires incident. I just hope nothing like that happens this year."

"Me, too. But listen." Jenny turned to face me. "Let's get to the good stuff. What about Doug? What's he like?"

I tried to play it cool—after all, Jenny knew perfectly well I was going with Alan—but it was hard to keep the enthusiasm out of my voice. "I like him," I said. "And Jenny, you know what we did at lunch?" I told her all about our picnic on the roof. Jenny was suitably impressed.

When the last bell rang, Jenny gave me a knowing smile. "You go say good-bye to Doug. I'll talk to Sarah and meet you in the hall in a few minutes."

I didn't argue. I went outside to wait, but although the halls were filling with students, Doug didn't appear. I couldn't figure it out. Gym class was over—in fact, school was over—so where was he? Didn't he want to say good-bye? Was he sorry he'd acted so friendly toward me? Was he afraid I was expecting him to ask me out?

Well, wasn't I? To tell the truth, I wasn't sure how I felt. Alan was my boyfriend, but it was hard to get excited about him. Doug, however, was different. He was so exciting—a little wild, a little dangerous, and very good-looking. But even if I was going to cheat on Alan, how could I do it with someone from Pittsford Central? Friendship and understanding between schools was one thing, but wasn't this carrying it a little too far?

Oh, well, I told myself, it doesn't matter, anyway, since Doug hasn't shown up. Obviously, he was avoiding me. Feeling regretful (and at the same time a little relieved) I turned to leave.

"Hey, Claire. Wait up!"

I turned around and there was Doug, still in his gym uniform. Wow! His legs were just as muscular as his arms and shoulders. Incredible!

"Hi," I said. "I just wanted to say good-bye. And thanks for showing me around."

Doug grinned. "P. C. is nothing. Pittsford is what I really want to show you. How about Friday night?"

My heart was trying to leap out of my chest and my knees felt like Jell-O, but I managed to speak. "Sure," I said.

Doug put his hand on my shoulder and smiled. "I'll call you." He looked at me another few seconds and then let his hand drop to his side. "Well, I gotta hurry. Practice, you know."

"Oh, I wondered why you weren't getting ready to leave. Practice for what?"

"Football," Doug replied. "I'm the new quarterback." He flashed me a dazzling smile and then jogged back into the boys' locker room.

I just stood there with my mouth hanging open, staring at the spot where Doug had just been. When Jenny came up behind me I didn't even move.

"Claire," she said, "what's wrong?"

"I have a date," I managed to mutter.

"But that's great!"

"Sure," I moaned. "Except for one small thing." I turned and gazed hopelessly at Jenny. "He's the quarterback of the P. C. football team!"

Chapter Four

Boy, sometimes I can really be a jerk! I mean, if I had given it a moment's thought I would have realized that Doug was on the football team. After all, he was wearing a football jersey, he told me he had played Pop Warner football, and all his friends were big, burly guys like him. But I had been too distracted by his good looks to think about all that. And now I had a date with public enemy number one—the quarterback of the P. C. football team. What would Alan say?

Jenny tried to be reassuring. "It's not your fault," she said, as we walked through Berger's, Pittsford's largest department store. "You didn't know he was on the football team. I didn't, either, and I always look at those team photos they print in the programs. I never saw him before."

"Yeah, come to think of it he told me he was the new quarterback. He must have been second string last year."

"That's right. Hey," she exclaimed, pulling a brightly

patterned blouse off the rack. "How do you think I'd look in this?"

"Good," I replied, barely noticing. "But Jenny, what about Alan?"

Jenny put the blouse back on the rack. "That's the real problem," she agreed. "But after all, Alan set up this exchange to promote friendship between schools. It just worked out a little too well." She gave me a crooked smile. "Pretty ironic."

"Pretty ironic," I agreed, letting out a sigh. We walked out of Berger's and joined the crowd of late-afternoon shoppers hurrying along the sidewalk. "Jenny," I asked, "do you think I should call off the date?"

Jenny considered. "I don't know. He's awfully gorgeous. And he sounds pretty exciting, too. On the other hand, you *are* going with Alan, and . . ." She stopped and looked at me. "All I can say is, considering how things turned out, I'm glad I spent the day with Sarah Filmore. It may have been boring, but it was a lot less complicated."

I had to laugh. "I guess you're right." We passed a homemade ice cream shop and I pulled Jenny inside. "I'm going to drown my sorrows in hot fudge," I told her.

"Good idea." Jenny patted me on the back. "Remember, when the going gets tough, the tough get ice cream."

Alan called that evening. We talked about school and my day at Pittsford Central. I told him all about the school and the classes, and a little about Doug, but I left out the part about eating lunch on the roof.

"Sounds good," said Alan. "I knew it would go well.

Now don't forget that article you promised to write for the paper.''

"Ugh," I moaned. "I was hoping you'd forget."

"No way. I also didn't forget about that new Richard Pryor movie you're dying to see. It opens this Friday.''

"Oh.'' Now what? Obviously Alan was expecting me to go out with him this Friday. Should I make up an excuse about why I couldn't go out with him? Should I call off my date with Doug? Or should I just tell Alan the truth? In the end, I chose a compromise. "Uh, Alan," I began, "I can't go out with you Friday night.''

"Why not?''

"Well, you know that guy I met at P. C. today? He asked me out this Friday.''

"What?'' Alan's voice rose an octave above its usual pitch.

"Well, actually," I said quickly, "it's not really a date, just a group of us getting together. You know, I couldn't really say no. It's sort of a show of friendship between schools. It doesn't mean anything. Really.''

I waited for Alan to react. Probably he would get angry, remind me I was *his* girlfriend, and order me to call off the date. Or maybe he would be hurt and beg me not to leave him. "I need you," he'd say. "Please don't break my heart.''

Instead, Alan completely surprised me. "It's your decision," he said quietly. "You have to do what you think is best.''

Strangely, I felt a little hurt myself. Didn't Alan care about me? Didn't he even mind that I was planning to spend Friday night with someone else? I wanted to ask, but I was afraid to hear the answer. What if Alan didn't love me anymore? "But this guy Doug is on the P. C. football team," I said finally. "What will the kids at school say if they find out?"

"That doesn't matter," Alan answered. "You know as well as I do that all this interschool rivalry is stupid. What counts is the way you feel."

"Yeah," I answered. "I guess you're right. I . . . uh . . ."

"Well, so long," Alan said flatly. "See you in school."

"So long." I hung up the phone and stared at it as if I could find the answer to my dilemma in the numbers and letters on the dial. When the phone rang a second later, I practically hit the ceiling. My heart was pounding as I grabbed the receiver and said, "Hello?"

"Hello? Claire?"

I knew his voice instantly. "Hi, Doug." My heart was still pounding, but now it was for a different reason.

"So listen," he said, "how about if I come over Friday evening around six? We can go out to dinner and then I'll show you around."

My mind began racing. I had to decide right now. Was I going to go out with Doug? He was handsome, exciting, and funny. Most of all, he was my ticket out of Miller's Creek.

But what about the kids at school? What would they think of me if they knew I was going out with the quarterback of the P. C. Ravens? And what about Alan? He said what counted was the way I felt. But how *did* I feel? I wasn't sure.

"Come on, Claire," Doug said smoothly. "Didn't we have a good time together today?"

"Yeah, but—"

"Look, it doesn't matter to me that you're from the sticks. Does it matter to you?"

I didn't really like the way Doug put that, but after all, he was right. Miller's Creek *is* the sticks, at least compared to Pittsford. "No," I said. "It doesn't matter."

"Then say yes." Doug's voice was soft and husky and I could feel my temperature rising. "I like you, Claire. I liked you as soon as I saw you. And I have a feeling you like me, too."

"Yes," I whispered. "I-I do."

"Good, then I'll see you Friday." Doug's voice returned to its usual relaxed tone. "Remember, six o'clock."

"Six o'clock." After giving Doug directions to my house, I hung up the phone and walked slowly to my room, dreaming about Friday night.

My dad may be a bit provincial, but at least he isn't as anti-P. C. as the kids at the Mill. He thought it was fine that I was going on a date with a boy from Pittsford. The only thing he didn't like was the idea of going all the way into the city on our first date.

"I don't know Doug yet," Dad told me. "I don't like the idea of you driving that far with him, especially at night. I'd rather you stay around here."

"But Dad, Doug said—"

"Humor me," my father said with a friendly smile. But when I kept arguing, the smile disappeared and he told me, "No more discussion, Claire. The case is closed."

On Friday afternoon I washed my hair, did my nails, and tried on about fifteen outfits before finally deciding on a white silky blouse, black jeans with a thin red belt, and the new red boots my mom had bought for me in Boston. Then I sat around my room, trying to do my homework but mostly listening to the new Michael Jackson album and thinking about Doug. I wondered if he'd mind staying in Miller's Creek tonight and what we could possibly do here. I didn't want to go anywhere I might be seen by my friends and that ruled out all the restaurants and the drive-in. Other than that, there was practically nothing worth considering.

When the doorbell rang at six, I leaped up and ran downstairs to answer it. I wanted to get to Doug before my father did, but I was too late. Dad was just answering the door.

"Hi," I called, hopping down the last two stairs and joining my father at the door.

"Hi," said Doug, shaking my father's hand and then grinning at me. He was wearing brown cords and a brown-and-white pinstriped shirt, the sleeves rolled up to expose his muscular forearms. He looked terrific! "This is some house," he said. "Really old-fashioned."

"It was built in 1801," my father explained proudly. "We've tried to keep it pretty much the way it was."

I remembered how my mother had always wanted to modernize things and buy some contemporary furniture, but Dad had refused, saying that Early American was the only style that belonged in a house like ours.

I glanced at Doug. He looked a little uncomfortable. "You mean no electricity or anything?"

Dad and I laughed. "Well," my father said, "we aren't all that authentic. We have indoor plumbing and a few other modern conveniences."

40

"Oh." Doug looked relieved and for the first time since I'd met him I felt just a tiny bit superior. He didn't know anything about life outside of Pittsford. He probably lived in a row house, just like every other house on the street. But my house was unique and I liked it that way.

"Well, what are you two planning to do tonight?" my father asked.

"Oh, we'll probably go to McDonald's and then the drive-in," I said quickly.

Doug figured out what was going on immediately. "Claire's going to show me around the area," he said.

It wasn't until we were out in the driveway that Doug asked, "So we're supposed to stay in Miller's Creek?"

"Yes. My father doesn't want me to go into Pittsford tonight." I shrugged. "He thinks it's too far for a first date."

Doug laughed. "Come on." We got into his car—a new blue Toyota Supra—and Doug turned the ignition. "Supposing we went to Pittsford anyway," he said slyly. "Your dad wouldn't have to know, would he?"

I looked at Doug, unsure of what to say. I didn't want to lie to my father, but I didn't want to stay around Miller's Creek, either. And after all, what could possibly happen in Pittsford? We were just going to eat dinner and drive around. So it was in the city instead of Miller's Creek. What was the big deal?

Actually, I told myself, Dad was being completely unreasonable. After all, I wasn't a baby. Just because he liked hanging around this dinky little town didn't mean everybody did. Why did he think my mother moved to Boston, anyway?

By the time I'd gone through the chain of logic, I was

convinced. "Okay," I told Doug. "I guess we can go."

"All right!" Doug turned on the radio, backed down the driveway, and started off down the road. As soon as he was away from my house, he sped up to sixty and didn't slow down until we hit Pittsford. I was pretty nervous, but I was excited, too. I liked driving fast, especially with the radio blasting and Doug by my side, but I was glad we didn't get picked up by one of the Miller's Township cops, all of whom were friends with my dad.

The first place we went was the Golden Dragon Restaurant. I'd had Chinese food before, but not Mandarin or Szechuan, which was the kind they served here. Doug seemed to have tried practically everything on the menu, so he ordered for both of us. We had Peking ravioli, which is little dumplings filled with pork and spices, and Moo Shu beef. That turned out to be beef and cabbage and all kinds of other things mixed together. We spooned it into pancakes and ate it with our fingers. Both the ravioli and the Moo Shu were delicious. The only thing I didn't like was the orange-flavored beef, which was incredibly spicy. One bite set my mouth on fire, but Doug loved it.

Doug didn't say much while we ate, but when we got the fortune cookies he slipped them in his shirt pocket and said, "Let's go. We can eat these later. I know just the place."

Out in the car, Doug turned on the radio, then reached over and took my hand. "Let's cruise around," he said.

I nodded. Doug's hand felt big and cool, and I prayed my own wasn't too sweaty. We pulled out of the parking lot and cruised through the center of town. It was getting dark and all the lights were coming on. Other boys were driving around, too—some with dates, others alone—and when Doug saw someone he knew, he honked the horn and waved.

"This is the strip," he told me. "I guess you've been here in the daytime."

"Oh, yeah. I used to come here a lot with my mother. She's in Boston now."

I was hoping Doug would ask me what my mom was doing in Boston. I wanted to tell him about my family and learn something about his. Instead he said, "Let's drive along the river. There's a great place to hang out there."

We drove past the high school and through an industrial section until we reached the river. Doug drove across the bridge and along River Road. The lights of the city looked fantastic from there. There were streetlights and lots of neon signs, including a big Pepsi-Cola sign that flashed red, white, and blue.

After a few minutes, Doug pulled off the road into a little parking lot. "This is the playground," he said. We got out of the car and walked to the edge of the cement. There was a chain-link fence around the playground and the sign on the gate read PLAYGROUND CLOSES AT DUSK.

"It's closed," I said, but Doug just smiled.

"Remember the ladder to the roof?" I nodded. "Well, this is much easier."

Before I could say anything, Doug hoisted me up and I grabbed the fence. He gave me a push and I was over before I could change my mind. A second later, he had climbed the fence and was beside me. "Doug—" I began angrily.

"Hey, don't be mad. Lots of kids come here at night. The cops don't mind. Besides, it's one of my favorite places and I just wanted to show it to you.''

Before I could answer, Doug put his hands on my shoulders and kissed me. Instantly, all my anger faded away. All I could think of was the feel of Doug's warm lips against mine and the soft pressure of his hands on my shoulders.

Abruptly, he pulled away and grabbed my hand. ''Come on,'' he said, pulling me across the dimly lit playground. He jumped on one of the swings and started pumping. Giggling, I got on the one beside him and took off.

Flying through the brisk evening air felt terrific. It had been years, I realized, since I'd been on a swing. I straightened my arms, closed my eyes, and threw back my head. When I opened them I was looking at the river, the city, and the Pepsi-Cola sign—all upside down.

''The municipal pool is over there,'' yelled Doug, swinging hard and pointing over the jungle gym. ''We'll go there some night. And over there's the band shell. Rock bands play there sometimes.''

The next hour was like a fairy tale. We went on the seesaw, slid down the slide, and made each other dizzy on the merry-go-round. Then we hopped onto the band shell and Doug pulled out the fortune cookies and handed me one. I opened it and held it up until there was enough light to read the words.

''Changes will bring both joy and sorrow,'' I read. Well, when Mom moved to Boston, I sure was unhappy, so I figured that explained the sorrow. But what about the joy? Maybe that would start now that I was out of Miller's Creek and spending time in Pittsford with Doug.

''Here's mine,'' he said, cracking open his cookie.

44

"Love is on the way." He looked at me and his dark eyes seemed to burn right through me. "Come here," he whispered, reaching for my hands and pulling me close. Then he kissed me, first softly, and then harder. His lips were crushed against mine and his arms held me tightly against him.

At first I felt excited, but when Doug's kissing got more intense, I became nervous. This was only our first date and I hardly knew him.

"Doug," I muttered, pulling my face away and looking into the parking lot. "I don't think— Hey, what's that?"

There was a police car coming down the road with its blue lights flashing. When Doug saw it, he froze. "We better get out of here," he said tersely.

I could feel my heart pounding against my chest as Doug grabbed my hand and led me to the edge of the band shell. When we peeked around the corner, the police car was gone. Doug let out a relieved sigh. "False alarm," he said with a laugh. "But I guess we better go, just in case he comes back."

I tried to laugh, too, but I couldn't calm down. Why had I ever let Doug bring me here? I asked myself. It was a really stupid thing to do. I tried to imagine what my father would say if I ever got picked up by the police, but the thought made me sick to my stomach. "Yes," I told Doug. "Let's go."

In the car, Doug turned on the radio again and started driving back toward Miller's Creek. Listening to the music, I started to relax. Doug slipped his arm around me and smiled. It felt good to be near him. His thick dark hair had been tousled by the wind and his shirt was open enough to reveal a few dark curly hairs on his chest.

In spite of almost being stopped by the police, the evening had been a real adventure. It had been exciting sneaking into that playground with Doug and it was great fun fooling around on the slide and the swings. And kissing him had been thrilling, even if he was a little rough.

When we pulled into the driveway, Doug leaned over and gave me a light kiss. "What are you doing next weekend?" he asked softly. "I'd really like to see you again."

I looked into Doug's flashing dark eyes. He was such a hunk! I was sure he could have any girl he wanted, but he wanted me. "I'd like to see you again, too," I told him.

"Then I'll call you." He put his arm around me and gave me another soft kiss. "Good night."

I got out of the car and watched Doug drive away. It wasn't until I turned to go in the house that I remembered what came next. Since Mom had left, Dad always made a point of waiting up for me after every date. He was really getting into his new role as a single parent, asking me where I'd been and what I'd done. Naturally, I couldn't tell him that Doug and I had spent the evening in Pittsford. I'd have to make up a story about all the fun we'd had in good old Miller's Creek. In other words, I'd have to lie. Knowing how thorough Dad's questioning was, I knew I'd better make it convincing.

Chapter Five

As it turned out, it wasn't so difficult to lie to my father. Once I got started, it was easy to invent a story, based loosely on a typical date with Alan, that included dinner at McDonald's, a 7:30 show at the drive-in, and late-night doughnuts at Dunk-N-Run. I felt lousy, though, and more than ever I wished my mother hadn't left. She would have let me go to Pittsford with Doug, and then I wouldn't have had to lie in the first place. I probably would even have told her about going to the playground. She wouldn't have approved, but she wouldn't have gotten too worked up about it, either. But being a municipal employee, my dad had a fit whenever he heard of anyone defacing or trespassing on town property.

In school on Monday, I didn't see much of Alan. We're in the same sociology class, but he was excused for a special meeting with Mr. Bower, and although we sometimes have the same lunch periods, Monday wasn't one of those days.

However, I did see Jenny, and of course she was dying to hear all about my date. After swearing her to secrecy, I told her everything.

"He sounds pretty wild," Jenny said when I'd finished my story.

"Yeah, I guess he is. But he's nice, too."

"Well, at least it's a change from boring old Miller's Creek. Are you going to keep seeing him?"

I shrugged. "I don't know. I have a date with him this Friday, but . . ."

Jenny nodded knowingly. "You'll keep seeing him," she said, and I had a feeling she was right.

The last bell had rung and I was getting my jacket out of my locker when Alan appeared beside me. "Hi," he said, grinning shyly. "How about a ride home?"

"Sure." As soon as I looked into Alan's earnest face, I felt guilty all over again. On the way to the parking lot, I slipped my arm around his waist. "How'd your meeting with Mr. Bower go?"

"Oh, okay. He's still down on the senior trip idea, but I'm working on him. I told him the exchange with P. C. was a success. The two P. C. kids who came here had a good time, too. Mr. Bower is really pleased with the whole thing. Of course, it was his idea in the first place."

"It was?" I asked with surprise. "I thought it was yours."

"No, he mentioned it first. But I arranged things." He glanced at me unhappily. "It seemed like a good idea at the time."

"Oh, Alan, it *is* a good idea." I stopped and put my arms around him. He looked so pitiful that I just had to say something to comfort him. "Listen," I said, "that date

48

was nothing. I didn't even enjoy myself." Alan looked into my eyes and I could tell he wanted to believe me. "Really," I continued, feeling like a first-class creep. "It was nothing. A big zero."

Alan smiled and tousled my hair. "Okay, kiddo. I believe you." We got in his car—an old Studebaker Lark that used to belong to his grandmother—and headed home.

"It's supposed to be nice this weekend," Alan said. "Why don't we go up to the lake? We can take the canoe."

"Okay. Great." Alan reached over and took my hand and I promised myself then and there that I would cancel my date with Doug.

The next day in sociology I got an unpleasant surprise. Our teacher, Mr. Ostrowsky, started a unit on oral history. He explained how much you could learn about the past from talking to people, and he played us a tape of interviews with former black slaves and read us the reminiscences of a one-hundred-year-old Minnesota farmer.

"Now we're all going to be historians," Mr. Ostrowsky told us. "I want each of you to find someone to interview. The person you choose must be over sixty years old. If you have a grandparent in the area, that's fine. Otherwise, you could try one of the local nursing homes, one of your neighbors, or if you're completely at a loss, you can ask me."

"Hey, Mr. Ostrowsky," Marty Baker called out. "I didn't know you were that old!"

Everybody snickered. Mr. Ostrowsky is young and good-looking, with curly hair and a mustache. He drives a motorcycle and the rumor is he spends his summers in Maine, living on a houseboat. "That's right," he replied in a shaky little voice. "I practically need a wheelchair to get to my Harley-Davidson."

The class laughed, but I was still thinking about our assignment. All my grandparents are dead, except for my mother's father, who lives in California. I'd never spent much time around elderly people, but frankly they depressed me. They always looked so fragile and sickly and it was hard to imagine they weren't miserable.

I thought about the time Jenny and I had eaten dinner at her grandparents' house in Pittsford. Her grandfather had had a stroke a few months before and he had to wear a bib and be fed like a baby by Jenny's grandmother. It was so sad. All I could think through the whole meal was that I didn't want to end up like that when I got old.

Besides, if there was one thing I wasn't interested in, it was the history of Miller's Creek. The last thing I wanted to do was sit in a nursing home listening to some sick old man talk about all the fish he caught in Lake Pawtaug in 1935. At the same time, I felt rotten for feeling like that. Someday I would be old, and I'd probably get a big charge out of telling some high school kids about my life.

"You can do this assignment by yourself," Mr. Ostrowsky was saying, "or in groups of two or three."

Well, that was a relief! Alan's grandparents lived in the area and they were both pretty young and healthy. We could interview them and it probably wouldn't be too bad.

When class ended, Alan grabbed his books and walked over to my desk. "Hey there, little lady," he drawled, "I sure would be honored if you'd consider doing this assignment with me."

"I think I could see my way clear to doing just that," I replied. "We can interview one of your grandparents, right?"

"Oh, let's not do that. They've only lived around here the last five years. I want to interview someone who's lived in Miller's Creek all his life."

"Like who?" I asked doubtfully.

"Like someone at the Valley View Nursing Home. My sister does volunteer work there, and she could arrange the whole thing."

"Oh, Alan, that sounds so depressing. Can't we just talk to your grandparents? They're nice, aren't they?"

"Sure, but they don't know anything about this area. Besides, they're going to Florida tomorrow and they won't be back for two weeks."

That pretty much settled it. Alan's sister helped us set up an interview with an eighty-three-year-old lady at Valley View and we were supposed to go meet her next weekend. It seemed I couldn't get away from Miller's Creek no matter how hard I tried.

By Friday Doug still hadn't called me. I was kind of relieved because, after all, I was just going to bow out of our date, anyway. Nonetheless, I was a little disappointed, too. I kept thinking about Doug's broad shoulders and ruggedly handsome face. I wondered what we would do if we went on a second date together. Considering what we'd done so far, I wouldn't be surprised if Doug took me parachuting off the Pittsford County Court House!

On Saturday, Alan and I went to the football game and watched the Mill beat Hansen Valley, 21–10. When the game was over, we drove up to the lake.

It was a chilly day and not many people were around. We paddled out into the middle of the lake and then stretched out in the canoe with our heads on a pillow and our legs draped over the seat. Lying there out of the wind, I felt warm and protected. My cheek was resting against Alan's head and his blond hair mingled with my brown curls. Above us, a group of Canada geese was flying south. I pointed to them and Alan nodded lazily, then rolled over and kissed my ear.

"So you liked Boston," he said.

I stretched my arms over my head. Right now the city seemed very far away. "Yeah, it was great."

"And you're applying to college there?"

"Sure, you knew that. Tufts, Simmons, and Boston University. And you're applying to Amherst and Saint Lawrence, right?"

"Well, I was, but now I'm not so sure. It seems to me I ought to get out of this area for a while, especially if I'm going to come back to Miller's Creek after med school."

"Oh, yeah?" This was news to me. Up until now Alan had always insisted he wanted to stay out of the city. I sat up on one elbow and looked at him. "What changed your mind?"

"You," Alan replied. "I want to be near you." Then he kissed me, a long deep kiss that made my toes curl. I ran my fingers through his hair and kissed back. With Alan I could relax and enjoy myself. I didn't have to worry that he was going to take advantage of me or push me to go farther than I was ready for.

"I love you, Claire," Alan said.

I felt a surge of happiness. Alan loved me! But when I

tried to respond, I found myself wondering if I felt the same way about him. I thought I did, but sometimes he didn't seem exciting enough. That's why I'd gone out with Doug in the first place.

I looked into Alan's sincere gray eyes. I could see a hint of uneasiness creeping over his face. He was waiting for me to say something. "I love you, too," I whispered and hugged him tightly. For the moment, at least, it felt right.

After dinner that night I went up to my room and pulled my stack of old fashion magazines out from under the bed. There had to be a quiz that would help me resolve my problems, I figured. All I had to do was find it. Impatiently I grabbed a magazine from the top of the pile and flipped to the table of contents. "Can You Trust Your Mate?" Forget it. That was the question Alan was probably asking about me. I selected a magazine from the bottom of the stack. "What Your Pet Says About You." No good. I don't even have a pet. There are a couple of stray cats that hang around our house, but my father is the only one who likes them. He leaves them chicken bones and leftover tuna fish, and when the female had kittens, he even went out in the field and sat up with her all night. I mostly ignore the cats but my mom absolutely hated them. She thought they were dirty, and last year when one of them sneaked in the house with a live mouse, she had a fit.

I stretched out on my bed and gazed up at the gingham canopy above me. If I squinted, the blue-and-white checks looked like the sky and I could almost imagine I was up on the roof of Pittsford Central High School, eating lunch with Doug. Why hadn't he called? I wondered. Hadn't he enjoyed our date? Had I done something wrong? Or had he just decided it wasn't worth driving twenty miles to date a hick from Miller's Creek?

With a sigh, I rolled to the edge of the bed and picked up another magazine. "Have You Outgrown Your Boyfriend? Twenty Questions to Help You Decide When It's Time to Move On." That was it! I sat up and flipped to the correct page. *Question One: Do you often find yourself thinking about another boy?* The answer was easy. I found a pencil on my bedside table and circled YES.

I heard the phone ringing, but I didn't even look up. *Question Two: Do you find you know what your boyfriend is going to say before he even says it?* Well, sure but— Suddenly it occurred to me that the phone might be for me. In fact, it might be Doug! Throwing down the magazine, I ran into the hall and grabbed for the phone, completely oblivious to the fact that my father had answered it downstairs.

Then I heard my mother's voice. "How's Claire doing, Bob?"

"Did you hear a noise?" my father asked. "Did someone pick up the phone?"

I knew I should answer, but something stopped me. I wanted to hear what my parents were saying to each other. Maybe they were going to get back together. I put my hand over the mouthpiece and listened.

"No one, I guess," replied Mom.

"Hmm. Well, Claire's okay. She went out with a boy from Pittsford last weekend. I guess she's getting a little bored with Miller's Creek."

"A date with someone other than Alan? My goodness!" They both laughed. "I wish I could have her out here again," Mom continued, "but things are so hectic. I have two papers due next week and I'm working an extra shift at the restaurant."

There was a silence and then my father asked, "Marie, have you thought about coming home?"

"Yes, and the more I think about it, the more I realize it wouldn't work. It's tough here sometimes, but basically I'm happy. I just can't handle the life you want, and you can't handle mine."

My father sighed. "I guess you're right. I want you back, but only on my terms. I know that's unfair, but I can't help it. I like my life the way it is."

"Let's face it, Bob. We're happier apart."

But what about me? I wanted to scream. Don't I have any say in this? Don't I even count?

There were tears on my cheeks as I carefully put down the phone. Quickly, I tiptoed back to my room, pulled off my clothes, and got into bed. When my father called, "Claire, your mother's on the phone!" I didn't answer. I didn't want to talk to her. I didn't want to hear her say that she didn't have time to see me.

When Dad came upstairs, I closed my eyes and pretended to be asleep. It was only eight o'clock, but I didn't care. After a minute, Dad turned off the light and left the room, closing the door behind him. I waited until he'd walked downstairs before I turned on the bedside lamp. Then I picked up the magazine I'd been reading and turned back to the quiz.

I wasn't crying anymore and I felt very calm. When I finished the quiz, I turned to the last page and read the results. *Count up your* YES *answers. More than thirteen suggests that you need a change. Start looking around for a new beau. Good luck!* I counted up my YES answers. Seventeen. According to the quiz, it was bye-bye Alan, hello Doug.

Suddenly it all made sense. If I didn't want to end up like my father, I had to get out of Miller's Creek—and fast. Clearly, that meant dropping Alan. He loved Miller's Creek and all that it stood for. If I ever wanted to get out, I had to stick with Doug. He loved the city and he knew how to have fun. Just like me.

I pushed the magazine off my bed and turned out the light. It was still early, but I didn't want to get up. Instead, I closed my eyes and listened to the night sounds—the hooting of a distant owl, the whining meow of one of the cats, the soft murmur of the television downstairs.

From somewhere inside me a voice asked, But what if Doug doesn't call? What will you do then? But I didn't want to think about that. Instead I thought about being in the playground last weekend. I could almost feel myself swinging back and forth, my head thrown back so I could see the lights of Pittsford. The Pepsi sign flashed upside down—red, white, and blue.

A moment later, I was asleep.

Chapter Six

Doug called the next day. "Sorry I couldn't call sooner," he told me, "but we had a game yesterday and then the team went out for pizza."

That still didn't explain why we couldn't go out Friday or Saturday night, but I wasn't about to argue. "That's okay," I said.

"You know how it is. I just made first string quarterback and I don't want to blow it."

"Sure. I know."

"So, uh, I'm going to be pretty busy this week. You know, practices and all. But would you like to come see me play this Saturday? We're up against Pendleton." He chuckled. "Should be an easy victory."

I didn't know what to say. The Mill was playing Hood Township this Saturday and I'd already promised Alan I would go. Well, not promised, exactly, but we never missed a football game. Never. What would Alan—not to mention the rest of the gang—say if I didn't show up? And what if they found out I'd been to a Pittsford Central game instead? I'd never live it down.

On the other hand, I reminded myself, so what? I'd already decided it was time to get out of Miller's Creek. What did I care about a stupid little football game? What mattered was spending time in Pittsford with Doug. That was where I wanted to be. What the kids at the Mill might think of me didn't count.

"Okay," I told Doug. "I'd love to come."

"Good. I can't pick you up, I'm afraid. I have to stay with the team before the game. But you can sit with my friends and we'll all go out together afterward."

I wondered if Dad would lend me the car. "Okay," I said, figuring I could work something out. "Just tell me when and where."

My father and I took turns making dinner and that evening it was my turn. I was just opening a package of spaghetti when Dad rushed into the kitchen and grabbed his jacket off the back of the door. "No time to eat, Claire," he said urgently. "Just got a call on the CB. Big fire over at McClintock's. Gotta go."

Along with being the building inspector of Miller's Township, Dad is also a volunteer fireman. Since Mom left, he'd cut down on his hours, but when there was a big fire, everyone got called. When I was younger, Dad used to take me along with him. Mom always thought it was dangerous, but I loved it. In fact, for years I'd planned to be Miller's Township's first female firefighter when I grew up.

But then something happened. Mom says I got distracted by adolescence. Maybe she's right. All I know is, I was never around when Dad got called to a fire. Usually I was out with Alan or Jenny or shopping with Mom. Suddenly I missed going with him.

"Dad," I said, "take me with you."

My father stopped long enough to stare at me. "I thought you were out of that phase."

"It wasn't a phase," I said indignantly. "I've just been busy, that's all."

"Well, I haven't got time to argue. Come on."

Together we threw on our jackets and ran out to the truck. Dad drove the back roads like a race driver, barreling through stop signs and never going slower than sixty-five. When we turned onto Cleary Road we could see the smoke. "Looks like a big one," I said, but Dad didn't answer. He just drove faster.

The McClintocks have a small farm on the north end of Cleary Road. They keep cows and chickens and they board horses in the stables behind the house. They rent horses, too, and Jenny and I used to ride there a lot when we were younger. It's beautiful land—acres of dense woods, rolling fields, and in the middle of it, Miller's Creek dividing east from west.

Dad tore up the long driveway and screeched to a halt behind the fire engines. "Just stay back," he warned me. I wasn't about to do otherwise. Years of watching my father fight fires had taught me to stay out of the way and keep my mouth shut.

While Dad pulled his boots and helmet from the back of the truck, I got out and took a look at the fire. The large barn was riddled with flames and smoke poured through the roof. From the nearby stables, I could hear the whinnies of the frightened horses. The other firemen were jumping off the trucks and unwinding the hoses, while chickens clucked and flapped at their feet. Above the noise I could just make out the frightened sounds of the cows that were trapped inside the barn. Near the trucks, Mr. and Mrs. McClintock stood watching the flaming barn, their faces tense with worry.

I hopped onto the hood of the truck while Dad joined the other men. They had turned the hoses on the barn and were edging closer, hoping to get in and free the cows. Dad was carrying an ax and in his firefighting clothes he looked invincible, almost like a superhero. I moved to the front of the hood and crossed my legs. I had my fists clenched and I was breathing hard and fast. Watching firemen is exciting, but it's scary, too, especially if your father is one of them.

While the firemen worked, Mr. and Mrs. McClintock came over to talk to me. "How ya doin', Claire?" Mr. McClintock asked.

"Okay. How'd the fire start?"

"Don't know. We just smelled the smoke during dinner. Hope we can save the cows."

We fell silent then as my father and two other men used axes and crowbars to open a hole in the side of the barn. When the hole was large enough, my father went inside. I tried to concentrate on the other men who were pulling the hoses around to the side of the building, but all I could think of was my dad. Was he okay? As the flames shot through the front of the barn, crazy thoughts flashed through my head. What would I do if Dad got hurt? Mom was too busy for me. I'd have to quit school and get a job. I'd have to—

Just then a big black-and-white cow lumbered through

the hole in the barn, mooing at the top of its lungs. Behind it came another, and another, and then my dad. Breathing a sigh of relief, I allowed myself to relax.

When the cows were out of danger, my dad walked over to where Mr. and Mrs. McClintock were standing. "The rest are dead," he said. "I'm sorry. But the fire's under control. Nothing else is in danger."

"Can't be helped," answered Mrs. McClintock stoically. "As long as the house is safe." I looked at the McClintocks with admiration. Those cows were the McClintocks' livelihood. Without them they'd be a lot poorer. But the McClintocks weren't the kind of people to cry over something that couldn't be helped. They were too proud for that.

Dad returned to help put out the rest of the blaze. It took almost two hours, and when everything was finally under control only one wall of the barn was still standing. The rest was nothing but charred rubble. A few wisps of smoke drifted upward from the debris. I helped the firemen and the McClintocks herd the remaining cows into the horse corral. Then we all went inside for coffee and something to eat.

After the cool evening air, the McClintocks' kitchen felt wonderfully warm. Mrs. McClintock made coffee, scrambled eggs, and bacon and we all talked and ate and laughed loudly. It was the best way to forget the fire and the twelve cows that had died in the barn.

On the way home, Dad turned on the radio and started singing along with the commercials. I glanced over at my father as he warbled a Burger King commercial off-key. He looked young and strong and handsome and I felt very proud of him. No doubt about it. He was a great father, and even though I missed Mom desperately, I had to admit that living with Dad was okay.

"You know, Dad," I said, "I love you."

Dad stopped singing and looked at me, first with surprise and then with tenderness. "I love you, too, Claire."

"But Dad, I gotta tell you. There's one thing about you I don't love."

Dad frowned. "What's that?"

"Your singing." I burst out laughing. "You're terrible!"

Dad tried to look offended, but pretty soon he was laughing, too, and when a Levi's commercial came on, we both sang along.

Saturday rolled around and I still hadn't told Alan I was going to the P. C. football game. Oh, I had planned to tell him, but something always stopped me. Either the bell rang and we had to rush to class, or there were too many people around, or else Alan would do something sweet and I'd feel too guilty to do anything except give him a hug.

Finally, on Saturday morning, I called him up. "Hey, Claire, hi." He sounded really pleased to hear from me. "Shall I pick you up around noon?"

"Um, I—"

"Should be a good game. Hood Township has a new coach and they're playing well this year."

I felt terrible. How could I disappoint Alan like this? I cleared my throat. "Um, gee—"

"Claire, are you okay?"

"No," I answered, feeling I was only partly lying. "I feel awful. I think I'm getting a virus. I'm not really up to going to the game."

"Oh, okay." Alan sounded concerned. "Well, get into bed. I'll call you later."

"Okay. But wait until this evening. I probably won't be up until then."

I hung up the phone and tried to forget about what I'd just done. Instead I went out into the backyard, where Dad was mowing the lawn. "Dad," I yelled over the roar of the mower: "Can I borrow the car this afternoon?"

It was too noisy for a conversation. "To go to the game?" Dad yelled back.

I nodded. Well, it *was* to go to a football game. Just not the one he thought.

"Okay," he shouted and then returned to his mowing.

I changed into pink jeans and a white sweat shirt and got into the car. It was a clunky old 1970 Buick Skylark. Mom had taken the Honda Civic when she left. On the way to Pittsford I listened to the radio and tried not to think about the lies I'd been telling. Loverboy was singing a song called "Queen of the Broken Hearts." Was that me? I wondered, and then forced the thought out of my mind.

When I got to the P. C. stadium, I parked the car and followed Doug's directions to bleacher section 8B. I was supposed to sit with the girlfriends of the players—a real honor, if P. C. was anything like the Mill.

I saw a group of five or six attractive girls sitting together and I approached them hesitantly. "Is Emily here?" I asked.

The girls all looked me over. "I'm Emily," answered one, a pretty black girl with beaded braids and large dark eyes.

"I'm Claire," I said with a smile. "Doug told me to sit with you."

"Oh, yeah," cracked a blond girl. "Claire from Miller's Creek. Sit down and watch a *real* football team play.''

Oh, great, I thought. Obviously Doug had been wrong when he'd told me all the girls were real nice. I could just imagine the afternoon turning into a nasty put-down session. But Emily patted the seat beside her and smiled at me as I sat down.

"Don't let Jane bother you," she whispered. She pointed to the field. "Here they come." I looked down and watched the P. C. team run onto the field. "Doug is number thirty-three," she said.

It was hard to believe that the heavily padded, helmeted creature was Doug, but when the announcer called, "Number thirty-three, Doug Landsberg," I clapped my hands and cheered.

Then the game started and the crowded stadium turned into an enthusiastic cheering section. The cheerleaders jumped and chanted and everyone around me yelled along. I didn't know the cheers but I figured it would be uncool and definitely unappreciated if I just sat there, so I did my best to scream "Go Ravens!" at the appropriate moments. It felt strange and a little uncomfortable cheering for the Mill's arch rivals, but what could I do? The girls around me were watching the game, but they were also watching me. I tried to get into it by forgetting about teams and just yelling for Doug. That seemed to work and by half-time I was practically hoarse.

"How about some food?" Emily offered and I followed her and the other girls over to the refreshment stands. Everybody seemed to know the girls, who obviously enjoyed their status as the players' girlfriends. No one talked to me, though, and I ate my hot dog in silence, wondering how the Mill was doing against Hood Township.

When we returned to the bleachers I got up the courage to talk to Emily. "I was just wondering," I said. "Who was Doug going out with before me?"

Emily pointed to the field where the cheerleaders had joined the marching band for a rousing version of the old Beatles song "All You Need Is Love." "See that cheerleader with the long red hair?" I nodded. She was leaping around like a professional dancer. "She and Doug were going steady but he broke up with her last month."

"Why?" I asked.

"He said she was too uptight." She laughed. "Doug's a pretty wild guy. He needs a girl who can keep up with him."

I nodded and watched the redheaded cheerleader perform a perfect split. I wondered uncomfortably if I was wild enough to keep up with Doug. At the Mill I had a reputation for being a little goofy, but I'm not exactly a maniac. Of course, since meeting Doug I had climbed onto the roof of the school and trespassed in a locked playground. There was no telling what I might do next. If Doug wanted wild, I vowed, he would get it. I wasn't uptight. Not me.

The second half of the game went quickly and in the last five minutes Doug threw a forty-three-yard pass that the wide receiver caught for an easy touchdown. The crowd went wild and the game ended with P. C. winning by fourteen points.

After the game, the other girls and I waited for the guys outside the P. C. locker room. They soon appeared, freshly showered and in a rowdy, exuberant mood. Doug gave me a kiss. "Great game," I told him and he grinned. I noticed he had a can of shaving cream in his hand and I wondered why.

"Hey, guys," he said slyly, motioning toward the Pendleton team's bus, "that bus sure looks clean, doesn't it?"

"Too clean," agreed one of the other guys.

"Come on," said Doug. Laughing and whooping loudly, the boys ran to the Pendleton bus and began spraying shaving cream all over the sides. A few windows were open and the cream dripped onto the seats. "Looks good," said Doug, and all the girls giggled.

A minute later, the first members of the Pendleton team came out the locker room door. When they saw their bus, they ran at us, cursing and screaming.

"Let's go!" yelled Doug. Dropping his can of shaving cream, he grabbed my hand and practically dragged me along after him. We took off around the side of the stadium with the Pendleton team in hot pursuit. I couldn't tell what had happened to Doug's teammates or the other girls, and frankly, I didn't care. All I wanted to do was get out of there, preferably without being beaten up!

When we reached the street I noticed Doug's Toyota parked beside the curb. We piled in and tore off down the street, leaving the Pendleton boys standing on the sidewalk, shaking their fists and swearing revenge.

I leaned my head against the window and tried to catch my breath. As we turned the corner I noticed Doug looking at me. "Hey, what's wrong?" he asked. "Are you okay?"

Sure, I was okay, but I was upset. I mean, the Pendleton team was probably feeling bad enough after the game without coming out of the locker room and finding shaving cream all over their bus. They'd have to clean it off the seats before they drove home. Sure, it was no big deal—I mean, it was only shaving cream—but it just seemed to me that the P. C. team were being lousy winners. It wasn't enough for them just to beat Pendleton. They had to rub it in by defacing their bus.

"I don't know," I told Doug. "That was sort of a dirty trick."

Doug frowned. "Oh, lighten up, Claire. It was just a joke."

"Yeah, but—"

"Jeez," Doug said angrily, "don't be so uptight."

Was that what I was being? And after I had just promised myself that that was the one thing I would never be! I looked at Doug. He was glancing at me critically, and I got the feeling he was trying to decide how he felt about me.

Suddenly I felt panicky. I wanted Doug to like me. He was a terrific quarterback, he was handsome, he was fun. And if I played my cards right, he could be mine. I didn't want to blow it, not when I'd gotten this far.

I forced myself to laugh. "Come on, Doug," I said lightly, "I was only kidding. Relax!"

"Oh," he replied doubtfully. "You looked so serious."

I threw him a provocative look and smiled. "I'm not always easy to figure out," I told him. "But believe me, I'm worth the effort."

Doug put his arm around me as we turned into the parking lot of the Burger Box. "I'll just bet," he said with a chuckle. "Now come on, let's go inside and wait for the gang."

Chapter Seven

At the Burger Box I ate a cheeseburger and fries while Doug and his friends talked about the game. I wanted to join in, but the conversation consisted mostly of inside jokes about the players and gossip about their love lives. Since I couldn't tell one player from another (including the guys I was sitting with), I didn't have much to contribute.

After a while the talk switched to school gossip, which I knew even less about. Finally, everybody giggled over the shaving cream incident and each kid told about his or her daring escape from the Pendleton team. Since that was something I could actually talk about, I made a point of throwing in a few jokes—mostly stuff about how funny the Pendleton guys looked when we left them shaking their fists at us on the sidewalk. Everybody laughed, including Doug, so I felt pretty good. I wasn't exactly one of the gang, but at least I had accomplished two things. I was going out with Doug and I was hanging out in Pittsford.

By the time we left the Burger Box, it was almost five o'clock. Everyone took off for the movies, but I had Doug drop me back at the stadium. My car was the only one left in the parking lot and since the only exit was barricaded with barrels, I had to drive over the sidewalk to get out. Doug wanted to make it to the movie theater before the show started, so we didn't have much time to say good-bye.

"I'll call you," he said as he drove off. I waved until his car was out of sight. Then I started home.

On the way to Miller's Creek I listened to the radio, hoping to find out how the Mill had done against Hood Township today. Fortunately, the DJ announced the local football scores just as I was turning into my driveway, so when Dad asked me how the game went, I could tell him we won. I even managed to make it home before Alan called to find out how I was feeling.

"Do you think you'll be well enough to go to the nursing home tomorrow?" he asked.

I had completely forgotten about that! I was tempted to tell Alan to go ahead without me, but how could I? The assignment was due next week and I had to turn in something. "I think so," I answered. "I'm feeling a lot better. Maybe this is just a twenty-four-hour virus."

"Okay. I'll call you tomorrow and if you're up to it, I'll come over around ten." Alan paused. "And Claire?"

"Yes?"

"I missed you today."

"I-I missed you, too, Alan," I told him, and the funny thing was, I meant it. In Pittsford everything had been unfamiliar and strange. I didn't know the names of the football players, I didn't know Doug's friends, I didn't even get half of their jokes. At the same time, everything had been surprisingly routine. Doug's friends went to the game, they went out for burgers, they went to the movies. It wasn't any different from Miller's Creek, except that in Miller's Creek I felt at home. I felt comfortable. And with Alan by my side, I felt loved.

The only thing that was different about Doug's friends was that they were wilder than the kids I was used to. Not that no one in Miller's Creek ever did anything crazy. After all, it was kids from the Mill who had slashed the tires of the P. C. coach's car last year. And two years ago, three kids (from the junior high school, no less) got suspended for putting a cow on the roof of the municipal building. To this day no one knows how they got it there.

But that wasn't my crowd. After all, Alan was the president of the student council. He wasn't exactly going to go around spraying shaving cream on buses—not if he wanted to stay on the good side of Mr. Bower and the rest of the administration. Besides, Alan just wasn't the type. He would rather paddle his canoe across the lake than cruise around in his car, looking for trouble.

The question was, what about me? What type of kid was I? When I was driving into the Burger Box with Doug, I thought I had it all figured out. I was wild, I was free, I was crazy. But that evening, when I heard Alan say he missed me, I just wasn't sure.

Valley View Nursing Home is about a mile outside of Pawtaug, on a hill overlooking the Green Valley. On the way there, Alan told me about yesterday's football game.

I tried to listen, but my mind was on the nursing home. The closer we got, the more uncomfortable I felt. I had no idea what we were going to say to these people, or if they even wanted to talk to us.

When we finally reached Valley View the first thing I noticed was how pretty it was. There were three buildings, each made out of natural wood and each with large windows on all sides. The next thing I noticed was all the cars in the parking lot. Did these people have that many visitors, I wondered, or did they drive themselves?

"They drive," explained Alan when I asked him. "They're not prisoners here, you know. And they run buses into town and to the mall for people who don't have cars."

"Oh," I said, feeling foolish.

Alan pulled into a visitors space and we walked inside. "We're from the high school," Alan told the receptionist. "My sister is Mary Ann Wallant. She set up an interview for us."

The young woman smiled. "Right. Mary Ann thought you'd like to talk to Mrs. Rosemont. She's a wonderful storyteller and she's lived in Miller's Creek her whole life."

"Great," replied Alan. I didn't say anything. What could be more boring than an old lady who'd spent her whole life in Miller's Creek?

"I'll just call," the receptionist said. "Why don't you have a seat?"

I sat on the sofa and read the literature about Valley View. The place sounded more like a motel than a nursing home. They had a gift shop, a pool, and a bar, and residents put on plays and volunteered in day care centers

72

in the area. While I was learning about Valley View, Alan took in the view out the window—grass, trees, a pond, and beyond that the valley and rolling hills.

"Claire? Alan?"

We looked up to see a tiny old woman rolling toward us in a wheelchair. She had short white hair, lively blue eyes, and a thin, wrinkled face. Surprisingly, she was wearing blue jeans and a brown-and-blue flannel shirt. Her thin hands gripped the sides of her wheelchair firmly and she wore a large silver-and-turquoise ring on one of her bony fingers.

"Hello," Alan replied with a smile. "Mrs. Rosemont?"

"That's right. What do you say we all go outside?"

Alan held the door and we followed Mrs. Rosemont down a cement ramp and out onto a patio overlooking the valley. While she turned her wheelchair toward the best view, Alan and I pulled over a couple of lawn chairs and sat down. "Well now," Mrs. Rosemont said, "what is it you want to ask me?"

"About your life," began Alan, flipping on the small tape recorder we'd borrowed from the school's audio-visual room. "Anything you'd like to tell us, that is. And about Miller's Creek. Mary Ann told me you've lived here all your life. What was it like when you were a child?"

Mrs. Rosemont laughed. "Well, that's a long story." She leaned back in her wheelchair and crossed her arms. "For starters, I haven't exactly lived here all my life. I was born here—well, in Pittsford, actually—in 1901, and I spent all of my childhood in Miller's Creek. But most of my adult life was spent traveling around the world."

Suddenly I was all ears. Mrs. Rosemont, it appeared,

was not a boring old farmer's wife after all. I leaned forward in my chair. "What did you do?" I asked eagerly.

"My husband and I were travel writers. He wrote on general subjects. My specialty was food. But Miller's Creek was our home. We had a house on Deer Road and we spent at least four months there every year."

"Where did you go?" I asked. "What magazines did you write for? How did you start?"

"Hold on," Alan interjected. "Tell us about your childhood first. I really want to know what Miller's Creek was like at the beginning of the century."

Mrs. Rosemont smiled. I could tell she enjoyed having an audience. "When I was born," she began, "Miller's Creek was nothing but forests and farms. It was real country. People from Pittsford would come out here on their vacation. In those days, it was a long trip.

"My father owned a dairy farm just outside Pittsford, but when I was five, he bought some land out here. Back then, everyone in the country rode horses. I didn't see a car until I was thirteen."

"What about Main Street?" asked Alan. "Were there many stores?"

"Oh, a few. A general store, a luncheonette, a bank. And later on a garage. My brother Sam worked there. There was one school for all twelve grades, and only twenty-one people in my graduating class."

"Wow!" I exclaimed. "And I thought the Mill was small!"

For the next two hours, we listened to Mrs. Rosemont. She told us about the job she'd had in the luncheonette and her first meeting with Howard Rosemont, the man who later became her husband. Mr. Rosemont came from

74

Pittsford, but he had gone to college in New York City. When they met he was a newspaper reporter for the *Pittsford Herald*. He did his first travel pieces on the United States and after he succeeded in selling some to the national magazines, the Rosemonts began traveling abroad. It wasn't until they went to Japan that Mrs. Rosemont got really interested in cooking and began to write about food. She was an expert on Oriental cuisine, but her secret weakness, she confided to us, was Big Macs.

The thing I liked best about Mrs. Rosemont—besides the fact that she had done so many different things—was her attitude. She was an enthusiastic storyteller but she wasn't pushy. It was obvious she wasn't trying to impress us or lecture to us, or prove how great she was. She didn't have to. She'd led an exciting life and she knew it. She was happy to share it with us if we were interested, but she wasn't going to force it on us if we weren't.

The other thing that impressed me was that Mrs. Rosemont was happy right now. She didn't act as if she thought her best years were over, and even though she liked to recall her youth, she didn't live in the past. She still liked to cook Oriental food and she still wrote occasional articles for newspapers or magazines. She had lots of friends at Valley View and two children she often visited. All in all, she was the most amazing old person I'd ever met.

"So you liked her?" Alan asked as we drove home.

"Yeah, she's great!"

"Well then, let's go see her again. I mean, you kept her so busy talking about her travels I hardly got to ask her anything about Miller's Creek."

I laughed. "Okay, okay. But first let's listen to the tape

75

and finish this assignment.''

Alan drove to my house and we spent the rest of the afternoon in my room, listening to the tape and writing a paper on what Mrs. Rosemont had taught us about the past. When we were finished, we had almost ten pages.

"Mr. Ostrowsky's going to love this," said Alan, leafing through the pages.

"I hope so," I replied. "I got a C minus on the last test."

Alan smiled. "Come here, Claire."

I crossed the room and sat beside him on the bed. "What do you want?"

"Just this."

Alan kissed me and I felt myself melt into his arms. He smelled good—like shampoo and cotton—and he tasted good, too. We stayed like that a long time until finally my father called, "Hey, are you two still up there?"

"Oh, Daddy!" I yelled down the stairs. "Knock it off!" My father had learned that trick from my mom. They were both pretty relaxed about what went on between Alan and me, but when things got too quiet for too long, my mother liked to butt in just long enough to cool us off. Now Dad was doing the same thing.

"Well, I have to go, anyway," Alan told me. "I still have other homework to do."

I looked at Alan and smiled. I loved the way his straight blond hair fell over his forehead and the way he tossed his head to push it back. I loved his slender body and his long legs. I loved the way he could be so serious and thoughtful and I loved knowing that I could distract him any time I wanted, just by running my hand through his hair.

"Okay, Mr. President," I said. "See you tomorrow."

After Alan left, I told my dad about Mrs. Rosemont. "Oh, yes," he said, "I remember her husband. They had an old farmhouse like ours. Nice people."

"We're going to go see her again," I told him.

"Good, Claire. Fine." Dad looked distracted and I waited to find out what was on his mind. It didn't take long. "Claire," he said, "your mother called today."

I could feel myself stiffen. I wanted to hear she was coming home, but I knew she wasn't. Was that what he was going to say? "Yeah?" I replied, trying to sound casual.

"She wants you to spend Thanksgiving with her in Boston."

"She does?" Suddenly I felt great. Thanksgiving in Boston! With Mom! We could go shopping on Newbury Street, eat out at the waterfront, walk through the public garden . . .

"One more thing," my father said flatly. "Your mom and I haven't made any permanent plans yet, but I don't want to drop any surprises on you. That's why I want you to know now. We're thinking of getting a divorce."

I don't know why I felt so sick all of a sudden. It wasn't as if I hadn't known. After all, I'd heard my parents say they were happier apart. Any fool could see that the next step was divorce.

But somehow I hadn't actually made the connection. I guess I just hadn't wanted to think about it. Now, however, I *was* thinking about it. And the more I thought, the more I couldn't help feeling that it was mostly my dad's fault. I mean, both Mom and I were sick of Miller's Creek. But Dad wouldn't even consider moving to the city. Why, he couldn't even handle the thought of modernizing our old farmhouse or driving into Pittsford once in a while. No wonder Mom wanted a divorce.

"Claire," my father said, "I know you're upset. Why don't you tell me what you're thinking?"

"No," I said angrily. "Besides, even if I told you, you wouldn't understand."

"Try me," he said gently.

I looked into my father's face and saw his curly brown hair, blue eyes, and worried frown. How could we look so much alike, I wondered, and still be so different? All he cared about were the things he could see around him—his home, his neighbors, his precious township with its ordinances and building codes—while I wanted to see everything: Pittsford, and Boston, and the whole amazing world.

"Claire?" he said softly.

"Can't you understand?" I yelled. "I don't want to be here. I'm not like you. I feel the same way Mom does. I want to get out!" Before he could answer, I jumped up and ran to my room, slamming the door behind me.

Chapter Eight

Dad tried to talk to me, but I went into the bathroom and locked the door. Pretty immature, I know, but what can I say? I was angry and hurt.

The next day I felt better, or at least not so mad, and I knew I should talk to my father the way he had wanted me to in the first place. But by the time I got dressed and went downstairs for breakfast, Dad had already left. I glanced at the note he'd left me. Something about a meeting with the township supervisor. I made myself a grilled cheese sandwich and hurried off to school.

You know how it is when you have to talk to someone about something unpleasant? Sometimes you can just put it off and put it off until you fool yourself into thinking it isn't important anyway. Well, that's how it was with Dad and me. At dinner that night, we both acted as if nothing had happened. The conversation was a little strained, but we managed to get through the meal without once mentioning Mom or the divorce or the things I'd said last night.

After that, it was easy to get through the evening pretending everything was fine, and then the next day and the next. In the end, we just forgot about the whole thing, but I could tell something had changed between us. I guess we hadn't been all that close over the last couple of years, but now we were farther apart than ever. I mean, we were civil to each other—even friendly—but we weren't really relating to each other. Instead, we were each off in our own little world. Dad spent all his time doing his job or hanging around with his friends at the firehouse. And I was kept plenty busy by the things that were going on at school.

Jenny was the first one to tell me what had happened. She cornered me at my locker on Monday morning and whispered urgently, "How can you look so calm? Haven't you heard?"

"Heard what?"

"Bunny Powers saw you in Pittsford with Doug on Saturday. She's out on the bus dock right now blabbing it to everybody."

When I heard that I hit the roof. Bunny Powers is a stuck-up cheerleader and one of the worst gossips I ever met. "What nerve!" I said indignantly. "Who does she think she is, anyway? It's none of her business who I date!"

"Sure, but if you want to keep any friends around here, you better stay away from P. C. football players. Besides," asked Jenny, "what about Alan? Does he know?"

My heart sank. "No, not about the second date, anyway. I was going to tell him, but, well, he's such a nice guy, I didn't want to hurt him." I sank back against the locker. "Oh, Jenny, what am I going to do?"

"There's only one thing you *can* do. Unless you want to end up a complete social outcast, you better drop Doug—and fast."

I knew Jenny was right but something inside me rebelled. No one was going to tell *me* who to date, I told myself. And that included the kids at the Mill. So they made me a social outcast. Who wanted to have them for friends, anyway? I had Doug. "I'll think about it," I said angrily. "But I like Doug. I'm not so sure I want to give him up."

"Hey," Jenny said quickly, "don't get mad at *me*. I don't care who you date. You know that. I'm just telling you what to expect from the other kids. They're going to give you a pretty hard time if you keep hanging out with boys from P. C."

"Okay, I'm sorry, Jenny. I didn't mean to jump on you."

"Oops, here comes Alan. Good luck, Claire." Jenny patted me on the shoulder and hurried off down the hall.

I couldn't read the expression on Alan's face. It could have been anger, pain, disappointment, or a combination of all three. It was probably a lot easier to read my expression. I felt sick. "Hi, Alan," I said weakly.

"Are you going out with some guy from Pittsford?" he asked simply.

"Well, uh . . . yes." What else could I say?

"It's not the fact that he's from Pittsford that bothers me. You know I don't care about things like that. But it really hurts to know you lied to me. If you want to break up, why don't you just ask me to my face?''

Wearily, I ran my hand over my face and tried to think.
Did I want to break up? I really didn't know. Alan was
such a terrific guy. When I looked at him I longed to run
my hand though his hair and comfort him.

But then I thought about Doug. I had only gone out with
him twice, but they had been the two most exciting dates
of my life. Something about Doug really appealed to me.
But to be honest, he was a little scary, too.

Alan, on the other hand, was much safer. Going with
him was comfortable, not to mention acceptable. Besides,
two dates didn't make a relationship. I didn't even know if
Doug was serious about me. But, on the other hand . . .
Boy, was I confused!

"Well, think it over," Alan said seriously. "But don't
expect me to hang around waiting for your answer." With
that, he turned and walked away.

The rest of the day was a real nightmare. Friends kept
coming up and asking me if it was true that I was dating the
quarterback of the P. C. football team. When I told them
I had gone out with him, they were shocked. "Does he
think you'll give him our football plays?" Jon Van Doren
wanted to know.

"Pittsford boys are fast," Suzie Baynor warned me.

"Be true to your school," Bonnie Davis advised.

And Jenny's boyfriend Ben asked me, "How can you
hurt Alan like that?"

Other kids were even more obnoxious. Some made a
point of saying "P. C. stinks!" every time they saw me.
On the way to gym someone yelled across the hall, "Wait
until Homecoming, Mason! We'll wipe the field with
your hotshot boyfriend!"

By lunch, I felt like public enemy number one. I actually considered hiding in the girls' room rather than face the kids in the cafeteria. Finally, though, hunger won out, and I slunk into the lunch line.

This was the day Alan and I had the same lunch period, and as I carried my tray through the lunchroom I found myself searching for him. But then I remembered. I couldn't eat with Alan—not unless I was ready to apologize and beg for forgiveness.

Well, I asked myself, why not? Anything would be better than this. But then I spotted Alan sitting with Bunny Powers and I knew I'd rather die than go over and sit with them. With my head held high, I walked past them and took a seat in the corner by myself.

I was almost ready to leave when Barry Fitch and Matt Rosselli came sauntering over. They're the kids that everybody suspects were responsible for spray painting the P. C. football stadium. I wouldn't be surprised if they were the ones who'd slashed the P. C. coach's tires, too. They can be real jerks, but because they're both good-looking and funny they get away with murder. Personally, I can't stand them.

"Hey, Claire," Matt began, sitting down on the edge of the table, "does he kiss better than Alan?"

I knew they were talking about Doug, but I wasn't going to lower myself by responding. I pushed back my chair and stood up.

"P. C. got off easy last year," Barry sneered. "This year we're gonna make them wish they'd never been born. And Doug Landsberg is gonna wish he'd never gone out with one of our girls."

"*Your* girls?" I retorted. "Don't make me laugh."

Matt grinned maliciously. "Well you can just tell your new boyfriend he better not leave his car on the street. Not if he wants to keep air in his tires, that is." Barry and Matt laughed uproariously and a few other kids joined in.

I could feel tears stinging the corners of my eyes. I wanted to say something—preferably something clever and sarcastic that would cut Matt and Barry dead—but I knew if I opened my mouth I would start to cry. Quickly, I reached for my books and turned to leave.

"That's enough, Rosselli!" Startled, I turned to find Alan beside me. He was standing with his legs apart, his shoulders rigid, and his eyes glued on Matt. His voice was low and dangerous as he said, "You'd better leave Claire alone."

Barry flashed an ingratiating smile. "Come on, Alan. We're just sticking up for you. You don't want your girl hanging around with some Pittsford bozo, do you?"

Alan took one quick step forward and grabbed the front of Barry's shirt. His eyes were flashing and I was afraid he was going to hit Barry. But a second later he relaxed and let his arm drop to his side. Barry looked relieved and Matt, I noticed, was slowly edging toward the door.

"Listen up!" Alan said loudly. Everybody froze. Alan put his hands on his hips and looked over the sea of faces that stared up at us from the lunchroom tables. By this time, a couple of teachers had showed up, but when they saw the president of the student council they held back.

"Now just stop for a minute and think about what you're doing," said Alan. "You're all letting yourselves get worked up over nothing. Can't you see how ridiculous this interschool rivalry is?" He paused and glanced at me. "Claire can go out with anyone she pleases. I don't care if he comes from the Mill or Pittsford or outer space. I don't want you giving her a hard time and I don't want you taking it out on the kids from Pittsford, either.''

Alan looked around. The room was so quiet I could hear Matt Rosselli breathing. ''Mr. Bower has already told me that any vandalism against P. C. will mean no Homecoming dance,'' continued Alan. ''And any fool can figure out it would blow our chance for a senior trip, too. Furthermore, if I catch anyone else giving Claire a hard time, he'll have to answer to me.'' With a final glance at Matt and Barry, Alan turned and strode out of the room.

As soon as Alan left, everyone started talking. Immediately the teachers moved in and yelled at everyone to quiet down. At the same time, the bell rang. A few kids started over to talk to me, but I grabbed my books and ran out the door. I had to find Alan.

I finally caught up with him at the end of the hall. ''Alan,'' I began, trying to catch my breath, ''you were amazing!''

I reached out to touch his cheek but he jerked away. ''I didn't give that little speech to make you feel better,'' he said gruffly. ''I was just doing my job as student council president.''

''But Alan—''

''You heard what I said. You can date anyone you want. And so can I, for that matter.'' For a moment his face softened and he said, ''I want you back, Claire. But only if you want me back, too.''

''Oh Alan, I—''

''Not now,'' he said, cutting me off. ''Think it over. Go out with Doug and see how you feel. Then decide. And this time, Claire, tell me to my face. Don't make me find out from someone else.''

Alan tossed his hair out of his eyes and walked away. I just stood there, looking after him and wondering what to do next. The hall was filled with students hurrying to their next classes. They all walked around me, making sure not to catch my eye. No one stopped to tease me, but no one talked to me, either. I was in the middle of a crowd, but I felt completely alone. Miserably I watched as Alan disappeared around the corner. Then I turned and started walking to my class.

Chapter Nine

I guess I should have been happy. For years I had been complaining that everyone at the Mill got typecast. You had a reputation and you were stuck with it for life. It wasn't fair!

But now all that had changed. In less than two hours I had totally wiped out my old reputation. I was no longer good old Claire Mason—a nice kid, talkative, a little goofy, and reasonably smart. No one even remembered to call me Queasy Claire, the girl who had thrown up on Prince Charming.

Now I was "the one who's dating the P. C. quarterback" or "the traitor" or simply "her." It was a new image all right, but it wasn't much fun. I was an outcast, the kid everyone avoided in the hall, the girl no one wanted to sit with at lunch. I was no longer invited to parties or asked to join the gang for burgers after school. Even Jenny was more reserved, although she did spend a lot of time on the phone with me, dispensing sympathy and moral support.

The result was that when Doug called and asked me to the next P. C. football game, I couldn't say yes fast enough. So I didn't have any friends at the Mill; so I'd lost Alan. Who cares, I told myself, as long as I have Doug. Why, maybe he would even ask me to go steady! I pictured myself spending every weekend in Pittsford, hanging out with Doug and his friends. It would be great, I told myself. In fact, it was what I'd wanted all along.

So for the next three weeks, I went to every P. C. football game. I rode to the away games on the P. C. bus. I learned the P. C. cheers so well I could recite "Ravens rule! Claw that school!" in my sleep. I memorized all of Doug's statistics and learned the name and number of every player on the team. I even tried to become friends with Doug's teammates and their girls.

The only problem was, I didn't get to spend much time with Doug. He was always busy with practice on weekdays and on Sundays he had to help out at home and catch up with his schoolwork. During the game I got to see him, of course, but the only people I talked to were the other girls. They were nice kids—especially Emily—but all they ever talked about was their boyfriends, and that can get pretty dull after a while.

After the games, I finally got to be with Doug, but we were never alone. Usually we went to the Burger Box with the other kids. Sometimes we all cruised around town, honking the car horn and yelling "Ravens rule!" and "P. C. is number one!" out the windows.

"Aren't we ever going back to the playground?" I

asked Doug one Saturday. "I thought we were going to sneak into the pool."

"Pretty cold for that now," he answered. "Maybe in the spring."

"Well, how about that Italian restaurant you were going to take me to? Or that disco, Flames?"

Doug laughed. "You're a pretty demanding woman, aren't you?"

"Well, I—"

"Yeah, I'm sorry, Claire. I've just been busy. You know, football and all." He put his arm around my shoulders and gave me a squeeze. "Hey, what are you doing this Tuesday night?"

"Nothing that I know of. But I thought you were busy during the week."

"Yeah, but this is special." Doug smiled mysteriously. "I'll come over around seven, okay?"

I looked at Doug and nodded gratefully. "Okay," I told him. "That would be great."

On Tuesday evening, Dad came home around five-thirty. It was my night to cook so I was in the kitchen, methodically peeling potatoes. "Oh, Claire," he said, taking off his jacket and smiling sheepishly, "didn't I tell you? I'm not eating at home tonight."

I dropped the potato into the sink. "You aren't?" I asked. "How come?"

"There's a township meeting at seven and Ellen Bresner asked me over for a bite before it starts."

"Who's Ellen Bresner?"

"She's the township supervisor's secretary," Dad

said. "I think you met her at the township picnic last year. She pitched for my softball team, remember?"

"Yeah," I mumbled. "Sure." I didn't really remember, but I could imagine. Lots of makeup, giggly, with long red fake fingernails. She'd probably had her eye on Dad for months, and then when Mom left she'd decided to make her move. "So how come she invited you for dinner?"

Dad shrugged. "It's no big thing. Just a quick bite, really. We both have to go to the meeting, so—"

"So *what*?" I practically yelled. Before Dad could answer, I dropped the potato peeler and stormed out of the room. Mom hadn't been gone five months and already Dad was dating other women. How could he do a thing like that? I asked myself. Pretty soon he would have this woman over for dinner and before I knew it, he'd be spending all his time with her.

I knew I was overreacting, but I couldn't help it. I missed Mom so much! Everything in the house reminded me of her—the pot holder she had hung above the stove, the Mozart record that still lay unopened beside the stereo, even the stain on the stairs where she had once spilled a bottle of nail polish remover. No matter how hard I tried, I just could not deal with the concept of my parents getting a divorce. How could they do this to me?

Dad came after me, calling my name and asking, "What are you so upset about?" but once again I retreated to the bathroom and locked the door. I sat on the edge of the tub and stared down at the black and white tiles. I'd planned to tell Dad that Doug was coming over tonight, but now I didn't want to. Why should I? He had forgotten to tell me about his dinner date with Ellen Bresner so why should I tell him about my date with Doug?

Dad knocked on the bathroom door. "Claire, this is ridiculous," he said wearily. "Let me in."

"Go on your date," I shouted. "I don't care. Mom's probably had a hundred dates by now!"

That remark was meant to hurt, and when Dad didn't answer I knew it had. I stayed in the bathroom and listened with grim satisfaction as he walked downstairs and slammed the back door.

After I heard the truck pull out of the driveway, I went downstairs, cooked up the potatoes, and ate them quickly. It wasn't much of a dinner, but I really didn't feel like making anything else. I was cleaning out the pan when the doorbell rang.

When I opened the door and saw Doug, I remembered that my parents never let me be alone in the house with a boy. But tonight I didn't care. I was mad at Dad and I was going to do whatever I wanted.

"Come on in, Doug," I said sweetly.

Doug sauntered in and sat on the sofa. He was wearing navy cords, a green-and-gray rugby shirt, and a brown suede jacket. As usual, he looked terrific. "Where's your Dad?" he asked. "I didn't see his truck."

"He's at a meeting," I said. "We had a fight before he left." I sat down next to Doug and took his hand. After all those crowded football games, it really felt great to be alone with him. Finally we'd be able to talk. And I had so much I wanted to say. "Mom's only been gone four and a half months," I began. "They're not even divorced and—"

"Come here." Doug pulled me close. "Don't worry, Claire," he said softly. "It'll all work out." Then he kissed me.

The kiss felt good, but it wasn't what I wanted. In the past, whenever I was upset about something, I talked it over with Alan. Not only was he sympathetic, he was smart, too. He'd given me a lot of good advice and I liked to think I'd given him some, too.

But now I didn't have Alan. Doug was here instead, and I needed to talk to him. Pulling away, I continued, "Did I tell you my parents are getting divorced? Mom's in Boston and—"

"Um, Claire, I don't mean to interrupt, but we've gotta get going."

"We do?" I asked, trying to hide my disappointment. "Where?"

"You'll see." Doug grinned. "It's something really far-out." He grabbed me and kissed me, long and hard. Then he put his arms around me and lifted me right up off the sofa. "Come on, Claire. Hurry up!"

I started to giggle. "Put me down, Doug!"

"Let's go," he replied mischievously. "Why aren't you moving?" He carried me out to the car and sat me on the hood. "Well, are you gonna just sit there or are you getting in?"

I laughed and got in the car. I was so curious about where we were going, I didn't even think about leaving Dad a note. As Doug peeled out of the driveway and started down the road, I rested my arm on his shoulder. It felt good to be sitting beside him.

Doug drove across Miller's Township and stopped be-

side a field on Windsor Road. "What are we doing here?"
I asked.

Just then two other cars pulled up behind us. "Just a
little paint job," he said, getting out of the car.

"Huh?" I got out and looked around. It was almost
dark now and the sky was filling with stars. In the middle
of the field, I could see the Miller's Creek water tower, a
huge green structure with flashing red lights on the top.
Behind us, Doug's football buddies and their girlfriends
were piling out of the cars.

I looked at Doug for an explanation. He was opening
the trunk of his car and pulling out some aerosol cans.
Then suddenly it all clicked. They were going to spray
paint something on the side of the water tower!

"Doug," I said urgently, "you can't do that! What if a
cop car comes along?"

"Not likely," he replied, slamming the trunk. "Besides, this will only take a minute."

While I stood there with the girls, Doug and the other
guys ran across the field to the water tower. A few of the
boys had flashlights, and as they shone them at the tower
I could just make out the ladder that ran up the side of the
tank. Someone hoisted Doug onto the ladder and while the
others waited below, he started to climb.

Nervously, I glanced up and down the road. Except for
the lights of a few distant houses, it was completely dark.
The other girls were whispering and giggling together, but
I couldn't join in. I walked away from them and got back
inside Doug's car. I felt sick.

Sitting in the quiet car, I tried to relax. It's no big deal,
I told myself. Doug is just going to write something silly

93

on the side of the water tower. It'll probably be too small to read from the road anyway. Besides, it's just a prank.

But I couldn't calm down. What if we got caught? Maybe Doug and his buddies didn't care, but I did. Miller's Creek was my town. Everybody knew me. What would people say if the police hauled me in for defacing town property? More important, what would Dad say? I wasn't even supposed to be out of the house!

Besides, it just wasn't right. Sneaking into a locked playground was one thing, but spray painting graffiti on public property was something else again. It was ugly. It was illegal. It was dangerous, too. Anyhow, if Doug wanted to spray paint a water tower, why didn't he do it in Pittsford? Why did he have to come to my town to break the law?

I was still stewing when Doug came back. He hopped in the car and turned the key in the ignition. "Whoo!" he exclaimed. "That was no picnic. I couldn't even see what I was doing." He laughed loudly. "On the last word I practically fell off."

"So what was the point?" I asked angrily.

"Huh?" Doug turned and stared at me. "Whaddaya mean?" he asked defensively. "We were just fooling around."

"Well, why don't you fool around in Pittsford instead of coming out here?"

Doug started driving. "Well, excuse me," he said sarcastically. "I didn't think that mattered to you. Pittsford, Miller's Creek—it's all the same, isn't it? If we didn't think that we wouldn't be dating."

"That's true," I said hesitantly. "But I still don't think it was a good idea."

"Oh, come on, Claire. Loosen up. It's just a joke." Doug reached over and took my hand. He smiled. "You should have climbed up with me. I had a view of the whole town."

"You did?" I asked, trying to imagine what it looked like.

"Yeah." He paused. "Wasn't it great that day we climbed onto the roof of the high school? You know, that's when I knew I really liked you. I could tell right away you were different from the other girls. You were daring. You knew how to have fun." He glanced at me. "I like that about you, Claire. Don't change on me, okay?"

Doug's words made me feel warm and happy inside. He likes me, I thought. He thinks I'm special. How can I be mad at him when he's so sweet?

"I won't change," I said. I squeezed his hand and smiled. "I think you're pretty special, too."

Doug let go of my hand and turned on the radio. "We're all going to the Burger Box," he said. "You want to come?"

"I'd better not. I have to be home before my dad gets there. By the way, what did you write on the water tower?"

Doug laughed. " 'Sultans stink. Ravens rule.' What else?"

"What?" I shrieked. "Why did you have to write that?"

Doug frowned. "Cool it, Claire. It's no big deal. It just gets everybody excited about the game. It's good publicity, you know?" He put his arm over the back of the seat and touched my shoulder.

"Well, I think it's stupid." I moved against the door where Doug couldn't reach me. "It makes everybody mad at each other. And if you don't watch out, you'll be in big trouble. Some kids from the Mill told me they're going to slash the tires of your car."

"They'd better not," Doug said threateningly, "or I'll knock their heads in. I'm not scared of the Mill."

I didn't answer. Doug kept driving and neither of us said a word the rest of the way home. When we finally pulled into my driveway I started to get out, but Doug put his hand on my arm to stop me. "Look," he said, "I'm sorry, okay?"

I kept staring straight ahead. "Claire?" His voice was softer now, and sexy. "Come on, Claire. I didn't mean to upset you."

Doug moved closer and ran his fingers over my cheek. I didn't move. Then slowly he lifted his hand and began stroking my hair. A warm feeling flowed through my body and I began to relax. I closed my eyes. Then he kissed me and I had to give in. I put my arms around him and kissed him back.

"There now," whispered Doug, "I knew you'd come around." He kissed my ear. "I just like to have fun." He kissed my nose. "Don't you?"

"Sure, but—"

"I like you, Claire." He kissed me again. "Will I see you at the game this Saturday?"

I looked at Doug and thought how handsome he was. And when he kissed me, well, how could I resist? "Sure," I said, resting my head on his shoulder. "I'll be there."

Chapter Ten

I was back long before Dad got home and when I heard his truck turn into the driveway I jumped into bed and pretended to be asleep. The next morning Dad was gone before I even woke up. Once again we had avoided dealing with the tension between us, and even though I knew it was wrong, I had to admit I was relieved. I didn't want to talk to Dad about the divorce and I certainly didn't want to talk about Ellen Bresner. It was just too painful.

When I got to school, I learned that Alan had called a special meeting of the student council. All representatives were supposed to report to the auditorium immediately following homeroom. My first thought was that the meeting had to have something to do with the words Doug had written on the water tower last night.

As soon as I got to the auditorium, I knew I was right. The meeting hadn't started yet. I took a seat near the back, a couple of rows behind Rob Thayer and a few other guys. They were talking loudly and didn't see me come in. "I saw it from the school bus this morning,'' Rob Thayer was saying. '' 'Sultans stink, Ravens rule' in three-foot letters across the side.''

''Probably the work of Claire Mason's new boyfriend,'' someone else said.

I leaned over my notebook and tried to make myself disappear. Obviously no one noticed me because they kept on talking.

''I'd like to spray paint *him*,'' Rob said with disgust. ''What a jerk!''

''I can't understand why Claire goes out with him,'' someone added. ''Can't she see how much she's hurting Alan?''

I scrunched down in my seat and considered. Was Alan really hurt? I couldn't tell. Over the last three weeks he had barely said two words to me. And Jenny had told me she'd seen him in McDonald's with the president of the drama club, Wendy Hill.

I looked up at Alan. He was sitting at the front of the auditorium glancing over some papers. What was he thinking? I would have liked to talk to him, but what would I say? Sometimes I thought I wanted him back, but other times I was sure I was happier with Doug. Besides, I had my pride. I wasn't going to beg for forgiveness, especially since I secretly feared that Alan might not take me back, anyway.

''It isn't so hard to figure out what Claire sees in that guy,'' I heard Angie Friedman say. ''He's a hunk!''

''Shut up!'' someone whispered. ''She's right behind us!''

Before anyone could react, Alan banged his gavel against the desk. ''Order, please.'' The auditorium fell silent and the meeting began. After the minutes and the treasurer's report Alan stood up. "I'm sure you know by now that someone vandalized the Miller's Township water tower last night," he said loudly. Everyone nodded. Obviously the news had traveled fast. "I called this meeting because I need your help. This year I want to stop this thing before it gets out of hand," he said firmly. "We have to make sure this won't be the beginning of another epidemic of vandalism."

"We didn't start it this time," Tim Smith pointed out. "P. C. is just looking for trouble."

"Well, I want to make sure they don't find it." Alan looked thoughtful. "I think we should form a committee," he told us. "You know, to make posters and announcements over the P.A. Something like 'Fight P. C. on the field, not on the street.' "

There were a few murmurs of dissent but Suzie Baynor said, "If that's a motion I second it."

The motion passed by a slim margin. "Great," Alan said with obvious satisfaction. "We'd better have a meeting tonight. Homecoming is only two weeks away."

Two weeks away! I'd been so involved with Doug and his friends I'd completely forgotten! I sat back in my chair and sighed. Who would have thought I'd ever forget about Homecoming? In the past, it had always been my favorite event of the school year. I loved the excitement of the pep rallies, the pageantry of the Homecoming parade, the thrill of the big game. I loved working on the student council float with Alan, and I loved sitting beside him in the bleachers, shouting encouragement to the team. And then there was the Homecoming dance—the biggest social event of the semester. Alan and I always had such fun!

But what about this year? I still attended the Mill but I was no longer a part of it. Things were going on without me, and nobody even cared. Obviously Alan had found someone else to help him with the student council float. Had he found someone else to take to the game as well? And what about the dance? Would he really go without me?

Well, I told myself firmly, I'm not going to worry. So I wasn't into Homecoming this year. Who cared? I had Doug. I didn't need Alan or the stupid student council float. And I certainly didn't care about the dance. It would just be the same old thing, anyway. Corny crepe-paper decorations, lousy punch and cookies, and the same dance tape played over and over. Totally boring, or at least that's what I told myself then.

But I had another problem to contend with. Homecoming wasn't just any game. It was the day Pittsford Central played the Mill. Normally, of course, I would sit with Alan and my friends in the home bleachers. But what about this year? Would Doug expect me to sit with his friends in the visitors' stands? I hoped not. Sitting on the P. C. side at other games was one thing, but I couldn't do it at Homecoming. It just wouldn't be right. Still, even if I sat on the Mill side, I was sure to get hassled. Maybe it would be better not to go to the game at all. . . .

"If anyone knows anything about the vandals who painted the water tank," Alan was saying, "please let me know. We need to stop this feuding before it gets serious."

I shifted uncomfortably in my seat. It was foolish, I know, but I felt as if everybody in the auditorium were looking at me. They were all waiting for me to rat on Doug.

Well, forget it! I wasn't going to get Doug in trouble, even if I didn't approve of what he'd done. Besides, maybe he was right when he'd said I was too uptight. After all, painting the water tower was just a joke, a way to let off steam. It wasn't worth getting upset about.

I thought about Doug for a minute and felt better. As long as I had Doug, everything was okay. Nevertheless, when the student council meeting was over, I grabbed my books and hurried out of the auditorium. I just couldn't bear to face anybody. I was sure I had guilt written all over my face.

Sociology was my last class that day and Mr. Ostrowsky handed back our oral history papers. "I really enjoyed reading these," he said as he passed them out. "I think we all learned a lot. I've made copies to put on the bulletin board and I hope each of you will read them all."

Mr. Ostrowsky slid our paper onto my desk. I glanced down to find the grade, but there wasn't one. All it said was "See me after class." What? Was it that bad? I looked over at Alan and caught his eye. When I held up the paper, he looked as bewildered as I.

After class, Alan and I walked up to Mr. Ostrowsky's desk. It seemed strange to be standing next to Alan after all these weeks of avoiding each other. I glanced up and found him staring at me. We both looked quickly away.

Mr. Ostrowsky laughed. "Don't look so nervous, you two. You both got As. The only reason I wanted to talk to you was to tell you how much I enjoyed your paper.

Mrs. Rosemont is obviously a fascinating person and your enthusiasm came through in your writing.''

Whew! I felt as if a two-hundred-pound weight had been lifted from my shoulders. "Gee, thanks," I said.

"I liked reading your different points of view," continued Mr. Ostrowsky. "Claire wrote about Mrs. Rosemont's world travels with genuine fascination, and you, Alan, counterbalanced that with your interest in her life in Miller's Creek."

"Yeah," muttered Alan. "Claire and I tend to see things a little differently."

Mr. Ostrowsky nodded, oblivious to the pained expression on Alan's face. "That's why you two work so well together," he said enthusiastically. "You each have a lot to offer, but separately I get only half the picture. Put them together, and it's really special."

Mr. Ostrowsky was talking about our oral history project, but I couldn't help applying his comments to our entire relationship. Maybe seeing things differently wasn't so bad after all. Maybe Alan and I needed each other to get the whole picture. I hadn't thought of it that way before.

I looked up at Alan. He was wearing one of his typical thoughtful expressions. His brow was furrowed, his lips were pursed, and his gray eyes were focused on nothing at all. I had to smile. I'd seen that expression on Alan's face so many times. Without thinking, I reached over and ran my hand over his soft blond hair, smoothing down a few stray strands.

As soon as I touched him Alan pulled away and I immediately dropped my hand. But Mr. Ostrowsky was still smiling, unaware of the tension between us. "I don't want you two to miss your bus," he said. "Better get going."

I nodded weakly and headed for the door, painfully aware that Alan was walking just ahead of me. Would he talk to me once we got out into the hall? Would he snub me? And more to the point, did I care? I wasn't sure. All I knew was that I felt nervous, excited, and a little scared— just the way I'd felt on my first date with Alan over two years ago.

As we turned into the hall, Alan glanced at me and asked quietly, "Why did you touch my hair?"

"I—I don't know," I answered, looking away. "I guess I was just thinking about what Mr. Ostrowsky had said. I'm sorry. It just seemed right."

"You mean what he said about our different points of view?"

"Yes, and about putting the two parts together to get—"

"Something really special," Alan finished. He stopped walking and looked at me intently. I could feel my face growing warm, and when I met his eyes my heart was pounding against my chest.

We seemed to stay like that forever. I tried to read the message in Alan's eyes, but all I could see was a question. What now? he seemed to be asking, and my answer was the same: I don't know. Then suddenly Alan smiled and said, "I think we missed the bus. But I guess we could walk home. How about it?"

"Okay," I answered, feeling suddenly elated. "Why not?"

We stopped at our lockers for our jackets and then walked through the doors into the crisp autumn air. The leaves were red and the sun was golden as we set off down Blackrock Road.

When I was younger, I used to walk all over the township. I knew every road, every stream, every good climbing tree, and the very best places to find everything from blueberries to wild flowers to toads. But all that changed when I got my driver's license. Why would I want to walk when I could be cruising around with the radio on? I would either drive my mom's car or get a ride with one of my friends. Except for hiking around the lake on summer afternoons, I never walked anywhere at all. No one at the Mill did.

Consequently, walking home with Alan was something of a revelation. "Look, Canada geese!" I cried as we started down the road.

"Yeah," said Alan, shielding his eyes from the sun. "I used to see them all the time when I played out here." He pointed toward an empty field. "Look at that."

We stopped a moment and watched some butterflies flit among the wild flowers. "Did you ever play along the creek over by Thompsons' farm?" Alan asked. "You know, where the older kids built that little bridge."

"Oh, sure," I replied. "Did you go there, too? I never saw you."

Alan smiled. "Hey, you forget. Boys and girls almost never played together back then. Whenever we saw a group of girls at the creek, we splashed them or scared them away with garter snakes."

I laughed. "You're right. But that never worked on me. I wasn't scared of snakes and I splashed right back."

Alan nodded knowingly. "You were tough. Remember that time in second grade I tried to butt in front of you in line? You punched my arm until it turned black and blue!''

"Oh, come on!" I giggled.

"Well, at least you didn't throw up on me." He chuckled. "That was third grade."

"Please, no Queasy Claire jokes," I said. "I can't help it if I didn't find your Prince charming."

Alan grimaced. "Ooh, bad pun!" He pointed to a group of split-level houses. "Remember when this was all woods? I saw a fox here once."

"Really?" We crossed the street and cut across the fields. "My dad saw a moose near the lake just last year."

"Come on," Alan said, walking more quickly. "Let's take the shortcut through the woods."

As we entered the woods, we both fell silent. Red and gold leaves fell from the trees and swirled around our feet. Birds hopped across the path. A squirrel scolded us from a nearby rock. It was quiet, cool, and beautiful and I felt good.

It was amazing, I reflected as we walked, how many memories Alan and I shared. Although we had never talked about it before, our childhoods were almost identical. We had walked the same paths, climbed the same trees, waded the same streams. We were in the same classes all through elementary school. We both knew Miller's Creek like the backs of our hands, and we both loved it.

Loved it? Me? Well, at that moment I did. Sure, Miller's Creek was a boring little town in the middle of nowhere. I knew that. But it was still my town, and as I followed Alan through the shaded woods, it felt good to be there.

When we reached the clearing, I could see my house on

the other side of the field. Alan lived about a mile farther on, closer to the lake. As we neared my house Alan asked, "How's everything at home?"

"Oh, okay," I replied unconvincingly. "I got a letter from Mom yesterday. I'm going to visit her at Thanksgiving."

Alan took one look at me and stopped walking. "What's wrong?" he asked.

I looked into Alan's concerned face and felt all my defenses crumble. My voice cracked as I whispered, "They're getting a divorce."

"Oh, Claire." Alan put his arms around me and held me tight. It felt so good to be near him. I rested my head on his chest and closed my eyes. Neither of us said anything, but it didn't matter. There was really nothing to say, anyway. I just wanted to be hugged and Alan knew that. He always knew how to make me feel good.

Finally Alan dropped his arms and we each took a quick step backward. Oddly, now that he wasn't holding me, I felt shy and embarrassed. "You want to come in?" I muttered, looking at my feet.

"I can't," said Alan. "I—I have to meet someone."

I looked at Alan and tried to read his expression. Did he wish he could stay and talk to me? Or was he eager to get away? I tried to guess whom he was meeting. Was it Wendy Hill?

Alan had a distant look in his eyes and he was biting his lower lip. He wants to go, I told myself. My heart ached but I thought, Let him go. It doesn't matter. I have Doug.

"So long," I said with false bravado. "I guess I'll see you around."

Alan paused long enough to meet my eyes. His head

was lowered and his eyes were dark and intense as he gazed up through his straight blond hair. He looked so handsome that my knees went weak and I had a sudden impulse to hug him and tell him I loved him.

"Alan—" I began.

"I have to go," he said gruffly. "Good-bye, Claire." Alan lifted his hand in a halfhearted wave and walked away. I stood there watching until he disappeared in a grove of trees. That was when I realized I was crying. "Alan!" I shouted. "Wait! Wait!" But it was too late. He was gone.

Chapter Eleven

After Alan left, everything seemed to change. The afternoon, which had been so cool and sunny, now seemed windy and cold. The red and gold leaves were no longer beautiful. Instead they reminded me that winter was on its way. Soon dead leaves would crunch under my feet as I walked out to the bus stop, and not long after that the ground would be covered with snow.

The thought of winter made me shiver. Turning up the collar of my jacket, I blinked the tears from my eyes and sighed. I wasn't crying anymore, but my nose was still running. I searched in my pockets for a tissue. Nothing. Sniffling and blinking, I turned and started back to the house.

I guess I must have been feeling something, but it's hard to describe what it was. Mostly I just felt empty. My chest felt hollow and the rest of my body didn't feel anything at all. It was like something was missing, but I couldn't figure out what it was. I was breathing and walking and looking around, but it all seemed like a dream. I wasn't really there.

When I got to the house, I walked into the living room and just stood there. I had homework to do, but I didn't feel like it. It was my night to make dinner, but I didn't care. For a moment I considered looking through the quizzes in my fashion magazines. Maybe I could find one that would help me figure out what was wrong. But even that seemed unappealing. If *I* couldn't figure out what I was feeling, how was a magazine quiz supposed to know?

With a sigh, I flopped down on the sofa and hung my legs over the armrest. Staring up at the ceiling, I tried to think. Okay, I told myself, so you walked home with Alan. You had a good time, too.

Well, that was no surprise. I'd had plenty of good times with Alan in the past. The question was, what about the future? Did I want Alan back? Sometimes I thought so. Like today, when he put his arms around me and held me. It felt so wonderful, so right. I never wanted it to end. Or later, when he looked at me with those soulful gray eyes of his. There was something about his expression that just tore me up inside. It was like for one second he had thrown away all his defenses and allowed me to see deep inside him. What was it I had seen there? Something told me it was love.

I sat up and rubbed my eyes. But what about Doug? I asked myself. If I went back to Alan, I had to stop seeing Doug. And that meant giving up a lot. No more Saturday afternoons in Pittsford, cruising down the strip in Doug's neat little sports car. No more P. C. football games, cheering for Doug as he threw a perfect pass for the winning touchdown. No more adventure, no more thrills, no more danger. I'd be stuck back in Miller's Creek again, doing the same old things with the same old people.

Or would I? What if I stopped seeing Doug, but Alan wouldn't take me back? Who would I go out with then? The kids at the Mill had ostracized me for dating a boy from Pittsford Central. There was no way they were going to forget something like that overnight. More likely, I'd remain an outcast for the rest of the year. And there I'd be—no dates, no friends, no fun.

The thought filled me with righteous indignation. Some friends! Those kids at the Mill were so close-minded, so provincial, so *dumb*, that they couldn't see beyond their own noses. In fact, the whole township was like that. That's why my mother had gotten out. She knew Miiler's Creek was a dead end, a complete zero. And I knew it, too. That's why, like Mom, I had to escape.

I was so caught up in my thoughts that when the doorbell rang, I almost fell off the couch. When I finally got up, it took me a second to realize what I was supposed to do. Oh, yes, the door! Someone was there.

When I opened the door and saw Doug standing there, I was practically speechless. It was as if he'd known how confused I was and had come over to straighten me out. I could almost hear Monty Hall saying, "Which boy do you choose? The one behind door number one or the one behind door number two?" And suddenly there was Doug, opening the door and saying, "Here I am. Choose me!"

The thought made me laugh and I could see the confusion on Doug's face. "What's wrong?" he asked. "Are my pants on backwards or something?"

"No," I told him. "I'm just happy to see you. Happy and surprised."

"Oh, well, I was just riding around and I thought I'd drop by. Want to cruise around?"

Why had I been moping around the house? I wondered. It was a beautiful afternoon. Of course I wanted to cruise around. "Sure," I said. "Let's go."

We got in the car and drove up Green Hill Lane. "So," he said with a grin, "how'd the Mill like my message on the water tower?"

"Not much," I answered honestly. "Everyone was really mad and Alan's afraid it might start a replay of last year's vandalism."

"Vandalism?" Doug repeated defensively. "Come on. We didn't break any windows or anything." He paused and glanced at me. "Who's Alan?"

I had made a point of never mentioning Alan to Doug. He never talked about his old girlfriend, so I figured there was no reason to tell him about Alan. Besides, Alan and I hadn't actually broken up—not really—and I was afraid Doug might get mad if he knew that. But today Alan's name had just slipped out.

"He's just the president of the student council," I muttered. "No one important."

"Oh." Doug turned the corner and I suddenly realized we were going to pass Alan's house. Naturally I looked up, and that's when I saw Alan, standing in his front yard with Wendy Hill. She was holding her bike and laughing at something Alan had just said. Alan looked delighted.

I closed my eyes and concentrated on not crying. My heart felt like it was breaking into a million pieces. How could Alan do this to me? I wanted to die.

112

But then I looked over at Doug. He had one hand on the stick shift and the other hand draped loosely over the steering wheel. His hair blew gently around his ears and his P. C. football jersey fit tightly across his muscular chest. What a gorgeous guy!

So, I thought, Wendy Hill is interested in Alan. Well, she can have him for all I care. Alan means nothing to me. Nothing. I'm in love with Doug.

I reached over and ran my hand through Doug's hair, the way I had so often done to Alan. But I caught Doug off guard and he pulled away in surprise. "What was that for?" he asked.

"I just like you," I said sweetly. "Is that okay?"

Doug grinned. "Sure it is. Hey, Claire," he asked, "is there somewhere around here we can go to be alone?"

"Of course," I answered boldly. "There's a fire road into the woods just ahead. Is that what you mean?"

Doug looked at me meaningfully. "You bet."

As soon as Doug turned onto the fire road, I regretted telling him about it. This was the place Alan and I had always come when we wanted to be alone. But it was too late to turn back now. Doug had stopped the car and was turning off the engine. Besides, I reminded myself, it was over between Alan and me. I could do whatever I wanted now.

Doug reached across the stick shift and put his hands on my shoulders. "Come here, Claire." Then he kissed me, lightly at first, then harder. Doug tightened his grip on my shoulders and pulled me toward him, but moving closer to him was uncomfortable; I was falling off the bucket seat and the stick shift was in the way.

Doug held me still closer and I looked over his shoulder

and out the window. We were in a grove of birch trees. Alan, I realized, had once read me a Robert Frost poem about birch trees. How did it go? But all I could think of was Alan and Wendy Hill, laughing and talking together. I felt sick.

"Claire," Doug whispered, "I want you to come to the Victory Bash with me."

I sat back in the bucket seat. "What's that?" I asked, trying to put Alan out of my mind.

"It's the dance we have every year after the P. C.-Mill game."

I had to laugh. "Victory Bash, huh? You guys are pretty confident, aren't you?"

Doug grinned. "Sure, why not? The Mill hasn't got a chance."

Doug's cocky attitude was a bit much, but I couldn't help finding it a little exciting, too. Doug exuded a sort of masculine bravado that attracted me almost in spite of myself. "But that's the night of our Homecoming dance," I said finally. "Why don't you come with me?"

"Are you kidding? After the Ravens wipe the field with your team, I don't think I'll exactly be welcome at your Homecoming dance!"

"No," I admitted, ignoring Doug's prediction about the outcome of the game. "I guess not."

"So come with me," he urged. "After the dance we're gonna drive over to the Flames. What do you say?"

Well, there was certainly no reason to go to the Mill's Homecoming dance if I couldn't take Doug. Alan was sure to bring Wendy Hill and watching them dance cheek to cheek would be too much to take. I might as well go to P. C.'s Victory Bash. At least I'd finally get to go to the

Flames, that disco Doug had told me about.

"Okay," I agreed. "I'd love to."

"Great!" Doug started kissing me again, and although it felt good, my mind kept slipping back to Alan. I thought about the many times we'd been down the fire road together and I remembered how my heart pounded whenever he kissed me. I thought about how comfortable I had felt walking through the woods with him today and how safe I'd felt when he'd held me.

But then I imagined Alan kissing Wendy Hill and my blood began to boil. Why should I feel guilty about being here with Doug? I asked myself angrily. Alan is with Wendy Hill right now!

Fueled by that thought, I threw my arms around Doug and kissed him hard. Doug seemed surprised at first, but then he kissed me back.

"And Claire," Doug whispered, pulling away from me, "you didn't tell anyone I painted the water tower, did you?"

Doug's words brought me back to reality—and that was the one place I didn't want to be. Reality—where Doug and his friends vandalized public property, where Alan made time with Wendy Hill, where my parents were getting divorced. If that's the real world, I thought, I'll take fantasy any day. I kissed Doug again.

"Claire—" he repeated impatiently.

"No, Doug, I didn't tell anyone."

"And you won't tell, will you?" He held me close and stroked my shoulder.

"No, Doug, of course not." He looked at me suspiciously. "Really," I said. "I won't."

"Good girl." Doug smiled and gave my arm a playful

punch. "I've gotta get home," he told me. "Mom gets crazy if I'm late for dinner."

Dinner? With a sinking feeling, I realized it was getting dark. Dad was undoubtedly home by now and was probably getting angry because I hadn't left a note telling him where I was.

"Right," I said miserably. "I have to get home, too."

But Doug didn't notice my worried expression. Casually, he started the car, flipped on the radio, and backed up the fire road, leaving a cloud of dust in his wake.

Chapter Twelve

When I got home, Dad wasn't there. The only thing I could imagine was that he'd gone out looking for me, so when I heard his truck pull into the driveway, I was prepared for the worst. Nervously, I went to the window and peered out, hoping to tell from Dad's expression just how angry he was.

But as soon as I saw Dad's face, I knew everything was all right. He was his normal relaxed self, and as the stray cats ran up to greet him, he smiled and stooped to pat their heads. Breathing a sigh of relief, I hurried out the front door and joined him.

"Hi, Dad," I said. "How was your day? Listen, how about going out for pizza? My treat."

Dad chuckled. "Forgot to start dinner, huh?" I nodded guiltily. "No problem," he said easily. "I'm late, anyway. Had to drop by the Petersons' out on Reading Road. They say a township truck ran over their dog." He sighed.

"That's the kind of important job I get sent on. Well, let's go."

Dad got back into the truck and I hopped in the other side. As we drove toward town, I realized this was the first time Dad and I had gone anywhere together since the night the McClintocks' barn had burned down. As a matter of fact, it had been a long time since we'd seen much of each other at all. Breakfast had turned into a casual affair—a slice of toast and orange juice on the way out the door—and half the time we got up at different times, anyway. Dinner was the only "family" meal and lately we'd taken to watching *M*A*S*H* reruns while we ate. In the evening, there was more TV or Dad would read or drive over to the firehouse while I stayed in my room and did my homework.

As far as I could tell, though, things were pretty much status quo in my dad's life. The only thing I wasn't sure about was his relationship with Ellen Bresner, but frankly, I didn't want to know about that. It was too depressing to think about.

I guess Dad figured things were okay with me, too. He knew I was going out with Doug and that I spent every Saturday afternoon at the P. C. football game, but that's about it. He didn't know anything about the trouble I was having at school or my confused feelings about Alan. I'd never told him and he'd never asked, so we just went on like that, pretending everything was fine. It seemed easier, I guess.

After a few minutes of silence, my father cleared his throat. "So," he began. "How's Doug?"

"Okay."

"Good. How's Alan?"

"Okay." So far this conversation was going nowhere fast.

"Gearing up for Homecoming?" he asked me.

"No."

My father looked at me. "Oh? Well, why not?"

"Oh, I don't know. I'm sick of Homecoming. All that business with the parade, and getting so worked up over a football game . . . It's just kid's stuff, really. Who cares?"

Dad frowned. "I didn't know you felt like that. Aren't you even going to the dance?"

"No. I'm going to the P. C. Victory Bash with Doug."

"Oh." My father was silent for a minute, thinking. "What about Alan?" he asked finally. "Aren't you seeing him anymore?"

I shrugged. How could I explain to my father everything that had been happening? How could I tell him about the soulful look in Alan's eyes and the comfort of his hugs, or about Doug's sexy shoulders and his rough, exciting kisses? How could I make him understand that Doug was my ticket to excitement and danger, but that Alan understood me in a way that touched my soul? No, it was hopeless. I couldn't explain, and I knew that Dad would never understand. Mom maybe, but not Dad.

"I don't know," I said finally. "Uh . . . maybe. I guess."

My answer was sufficiently uncommunicative to turn Dad off. He didn't ask me anything else for the rest of the drive and I just stared out the window, watching the trees and houses pass by.

At the Town Pizzeria, we ordered a large pepperoni and

mushroom and made polite conversation while we waited. Dad told me about what was going on in the township. A housing development was being built about a mile from the lake and the McClintocks had rebuilt their barn. I told him I'd gotten an A on my oral history project.

"That's great," he said. "And did you go back and see Mrs. Rosemont again?"

"No. I meant to, but . . ." Funny, but I just hadn't thought of it. I guess I'd been too busy. Besides, visiting Mrs. Rosemont would only remind me of Alan and I didn't need that. It was over between Alan and me, and the less I thought about him, the better.

"You should," Dad was saying. "I'll bet she'd like to see you. How about Alan? Has he been there?"

I shrugged. "I don't know and I don't care."

Dad frowned. "I don't get it. Just what's going on between you and Alan?"

"Nothing," I said irritably. "We broke up. Okay?"

"Oh, Claire," Dad said sadly. "What a shame. Alan is such a great guy."

Typical, I thought. Alan is my father's idea of a great guy because the two of them are exactly alike. They're both small town people who think Miller's Creek is some kind of paradise. Yuck! "Alan is strictly small-time," I muttered. "Just like you."

I regretted my words as soon as I said them. Sometimes I can be pretty thoughtless, but this was going too far. "I'm sorry," I said in a little voice. "I didn't mean that. Really."

Dad looked down at the table as the waitress brought our pizza. For a long time he didn't say anything. Then finally he looked at me, a pained expression on his face.

For a second I thought he was going to cry. Why hadn't I just kept my mouth shut? I thought miserably. Why had I said anything at all?

"Claire," my father began, "I've been thinking. You know, your mom and I thought it would be best for you to spend your senior year in Miller's Creek. We didn't want to tear you away from your friends, and besides, your mother wasn't in any position to take care of you."

I waited—worried and uncertain—while Dad sipped his soda. "But now, I don't know," he continued. "You're not happy here—that's obvious. You're going out with a boy from another school, you're not involved in your own school activities, you're barely talking to me. Maybe it would be better if you finished the last half of the year in Boston. It wouldn't be easy, but if I sent your mom some money . . ."

My mind was reeling. Did Dad really want me to finish high school in Boston? My first thought was that he wanted to get rid of me so he could spend more time with Ellen Bresner. But no, that was ridiculous. Dad was just responding to what I'd been feeling. After all, I *did* want to move to Boston, didn't I?

I tried to imagine what it would be like living with my mother. There wasn't much room in that house she was sharing. Would I have to sleep in the same room as Mom and share the bathroom with five other people? And what about high school? By the time I learned my way around, the year would be over. How would I ever make any friends?

Hold on, Claire, I told myself. Calm down. Living with Mom in Boston is exactly what you wanted. Just think of it—hanging out in the city with Mom and her friends, walking her dog in the park, staying up late watching *Saturday Night Live*, eating out. Think of all the hip kids I could meet, the great dates I'd have, the rock clubs I'd go to. It would be great!

"Well," I said finally, "sure. I mean, if it's okay with you and Mom . . . I guess so. Why not?"

Dad looked at his slice of pizza as if it were the most interesting thing he'd ever seen. "Okay," he said quietly. "I'll talk to your mother and see what she thinks."

On the way home, neither Dad nor I said anything for a long time. Then, suddenly, Dad slowed down and pointed out the window. "See that house?" he said. There was a little white farmhouse on the right. "Your mom and I considered buying that once. We thought we might like a farm."

"You did?" I asked incredulously. I tried to imagine myself living on a farm, with cows and pigs and chickens. A lot of kids in my school *did* live on farms and I remembered when I was little I used to envy them. While I came to "show and tell" with a new doll or an oddly shaped acorn, they brought eggs that we watched hatch into baby chickens. I always wanted to bring one home, but Mom said no.

"But it didn't work out," Dad was saying. "I got offered a job with the township and that was a lot more secure."

"What did you do before that?" It seemed to me my father had been a building inspector forever.

"Odd jobs," Dad replied. "I worked in a hardware store, I mowed lawns, I even worked as a lumberjack in Canada for a while. Before that I mostly bummed around. I drove cross-country with a friend of mine from school."

Wow! I had never thought of my father as anything but a plain old dad before now. It was hard to imagine him chopping down trees or driving cross-country. "What kind of bumming around?" I asked.

Dad chuckled. "Well, did you ever hear of Jack Kerouac? He wrote a novel called *On the Road*. My friend Bob Bartholemew and I loved that book and we decided to drive the same route the characters in the book had followed." He shook his head, remembering.

Now I was really interested. "What was it like?"

"Pretty crazy," he said. "We were so poor we had to sleep in the back of the car. Practically all we ate were hamburgers. By the time we got to California we were so broke, we had to call our folks and beg for money. Then we sold our car and took a plane back home."

I was so interested in what Dad was saying that I hardly noticed when he turned into our driveway. "Tell me more," I said.

"Okay. Let's go in and make some coffee." We got out of the truck but Dad just stood there, staring up at the house. The outside light was on, illuminating the wooden porch, the brown stone walls, and the front windows with their white shutters. "I love this house," my father said softly. He smiled. "Remember how the floors slanted when we first moved in?"

"Sure. I used to roll my marbles across it. And there was a crack along the floorboard in the kitchen where I used to hide things. Pennies and yarn and stuff."

Dad laughed. "It took a lot of work to fix this place up. But it was worth it."

We walked inside and I put up the water for the coffee. "Claire," Dad said, "you know what? Last weekend

123

when I was mowing the lawn I suddenly remembered that treehouse I built for you. Remember? It was at the very back of the lot.''

Sure I remembered. I used to go up there all the time when I wanted to be alone to think and dream. I used to pretend the backyard was my magic kingdom and the treehouse was my castle. I loved it up there. ''Yeah. I haven't been back there for years.''

''It's still there,'' Dad told me. ''A little worse for wear, but still standing. You used to love that place.''

Dad and I spent the rest of the evening sitting around the kitchen and talking. We were careful not to touch on any unpleasant topics like Doug or Alan or the possibility of me moving to Boston, but we still had a lot to say. Dad told me about his cross-country adventures and we both reminisced about my childhood and our house and our lives in Miller's Creek. It was the most we'd talked to each other in the last three months and it was really nice.

When we finally decided to call it quits, it was almost midnight. ''By the way,'' Dad asked me, ''where's the mail?''

''Oh, I forgot to bring it in.'' I didn't mention that I'd been out with Doug that afternoon or that I'd walked home from school with Alan.

Dad went out to the mailbox and came back with a stack of letters. ''One for you, Claire. From your mom.''

I took the letter and kissed Dad good night. Upstairs I brushed my teeth and thought about all the things Dad and I had talked about. Over the years, I'd heard a few things about Dad's childhood, but never anything about his adult life. To tell the truth, it had never occurred to me that he'd even *had* a life before he'd married Mom and they'd had

124

me. But now I had to admit, Dad was a pretty interesting guy. I wondered what other stories he had to tell.

I got into bed and read Mom's letter. It was short and chatty, all about how much she was enjoying autumn in Boston and how crazy it was to be back in school after so many years. She told me she had waited on two members of the J. Geils Band at the vegetarian restaurant and she'd gotten their autographs for me. And she said she couldn't wait until Thanksgiving so we could be together again.

All evening I had been a part of Dad's world, but now, as I folded Mom's letter and slipped it back in the envelope, I felt myself being drawn to Boston again. The stores, the restaurants, the lights, the people. Maybe I *should* finish my senior year in Boston, even if it did mean leaving Miller's Creek. And Doug . . . and Dad . . . and Alan . . .

I turned out the light and saw their faces swimming before my eyes. Mom, Dad, Doug, Alan in an endless circle. Whom should I pick? What did I want? Where was I supposed to be? The questions were still unanswered when I finally fell asleep.

Chapter Thirteen

～～

During the next couple of weeks Dad was pretty busy.
There was a new zoning law being considered by the town
council and that meant a lot of meetings, plus the fire
department wanted to open a new station house and Dad
was involved in that. Consequently, Dad and I pretty
much fell back into our old routine of quick breakfasts,
dinner in front of the television (if Dad even made it home
for dinner), and busy evenings in separate rooms. From
my point of view, the return to our old schedule was both
good and bad. The bad part was I didn't get to learn
anything else about Dad's life. The good part was we
didn't have time to talk about my possible move to Boston, either.

The reason that was good was because I was still extremely confused. I *thought* I wanted to go to Boston—
after all, I'd spent the last three months whining about
how much I hated Miller's Creek. But whenever I tried to

imagine myself living with Mom and going to high school in Boston, I felt worried and uneasy. I guess it was just the idea of leaving something comfortable and familiar for something new and uncertain. It didn't matter that the new and uncertain would probably be wonderful and exciting, too. I was still nervous.

Meanwhile, in school everyone was busy except me. They were all making floats for the Homecoming parade and putting up decorations for the Homecoming dance. The football team, the cheerleaders, and the marching band were practicing every day after school. The girls were all driving to the mall or into Pittsford to buy new clothes for the dance and the boys were making reservations at fancy restaurants for dinner.

Alan's campaign against football vandalism was in full swing. There were posters all over the school reminding the Mill to "Stay cool, don't break the rules!" and "Fight P. C. on the field, not on the street!" So far the campaign had been a complete success. Since Doug and his buddies had spray painted the water tower, no further vandalism had occurred. The administration was delighted and Mr. Bower was so happy he was considering giving Alan permission to organize a senior trip.

In fact, everyone was happy except me. All these activities were going on around me but I could only stand on the fringes and watch. No one wanted me to be involved and I had too much pride to ask. Instead, I told myself that I wasn't interested in Homecoming or anything else that went on at the Mill. I was above all that.

The only problem was, I wasn't a part of Pittsford Central, either. I couldn't help put up decorations for the Victory Bash because I wasn't a P. C. student. I couldn't go to the football practices because Doug didn't want me to. "You'd just break my concentration," he said. In fact, I couldn't see Doug at all. "I'm awfully busy," he told me on the phone. "But we'll see each other at the dance. Okay?" Well, what could I say? I didn't like it, but Doug promised me we'd have lots of time together after football season was over, so I tried to console myself with that.

Then one afternoon, a few days before Homecoming, Jenny called me and asked if I was going to the pep rally.

"What pep rally?" I asked blankly.

"Are you putting me on?" she asked in astonishment. "*The* pep rally. The one we always have before Homecoming. You do remember what Homecoming is, don't you?"

"All right, cut the sarcasm. I just forgot. I'm not really into Homecoming this year. You know that."

"I know. I still can't believe you're going to a dance at P. C. instead of the Homecoming dance. What if P. C. wins the game? They'll be gloating all evening. How will you stand it?"

"Well, it'll be better than watching Alan dance cheek to cheek with Wendy Hill," I answered. "I'd rather spend the evening in quicksand than watch that, thank you."

"You don't know for sure he's taking Wendy," Jenny said. "But we've been through all this before. What I really want to know is this: Are you coming to the game?"

"I guess so." Actually, I hadn't really decided. Sitting on the P. C. side seemed wrong, but sitting in the Mill bleachers didn't sound right, either. Maybe I could rent a helicopter and hover above the stadium, right over the middle of the field.

"Well, you have to come to the pep rally," Jenny

129

continued. "It's tonight and I need a ride. Come on, Claire. Please?"

"Well, I—"

"Look, Claire, are we friends or what? Mom needs the car tonight and Dad's car is in the shop. I called four other kids and none of them are home."

Well, what could I say? Jenny's my best friend. She's practically the only kid in the whole school who hadn't freaked out when I'd started dating Doug. At this point, she was the only friend I had. "Okay," I told her. "When do you want me to pick you up?"

"Seven o'clock. And thanks, Claire. You're a real friend. Bye!"

When we got to the high school, the parking lot was already crowded with students. A couple of kids with station wagons had brought soda and food and were partying around their tailgates. From inside, the marching band could be heard blasting through our alma mater, "Miller's Township, Ere We Hail." Members of the pep club were hurrying into the school, carrying their pom-poms and wearing their black-and-gold sweaters.

Much as I tried to act uninterested, I couldn't help feeling a little excited. I love pep rallies—the noise, the energy, the school spirit. And this was my school. Miller's Township, ere we hail. Just hearing the alma mater seemed to stir something inside me. I wanted to rush inside and start cheering.

But how could I? Nobody wanted me there. I was a traitor, an outcast. Besides, I couldn't possibly join in a cheer that went "Raise the bow and aim the arrow, Shoot the Ravens from the sky. Miller's Township, we're the leaders, Pittsford Central, you must die!'' That would be disloyal to Doug.

"I'm so psyched!" Jenny exclaimed when I stopped the car. "Let's go in."

"Oh, I don't know," I told her. "Maybe I'll just drive around and pick you up later."

Jenny looked shocked. "Claire, come on! We've gone to the Homecoming pep rally together every year since seventh grade. You can't just drive around. Where will you go?"

"I don't know." Jenny had opened the door and the cool night air made me shiver. The lights from the gym looked warm and inviting, and when I heard the marching band swing into the Mill's fight song, I could feel myself weakening.

Jenny ran around to my side and opened the door. "Hurry up! It's almost seven-thirty."

"Oh, all right." I got out and followed Jenny into the school. In the gym, the bleachers were filled with kids, clapping along to the marching band music. The pep club sat next to the band, shaking their pom-poms and singing enthusiastically. The cheerleaders were in the front row and behind them sat the members of the football team. Alan and Mr. Bower were sitting on folding chairs at the front of the gym. A podium with a microphone had been set up and the whole thing was draped with black-and-gold streamers.

As we walked into the gym, the marching band had just finished the fight song and the place was relatively quiet. Jenny and I grabbed the first available seats and I prayed no one had noticed me. But then I heard a voice behind me, exclaiming in a loud stage whisper, "Guess they wouldn't let you into the P. C. pep rally, huh, Mason?'' I could feel my face turning red, but I didn't turn around, and before anyone else could make a comment, the marching band launched into another song.

After the band finished its number there was a brief welcome by Mr. Bower and the head cheerleader introduced the football team. Then the cheers began. At first I felt really inhibited. I was sure everyone was looking at me, and I had this horrible vision of all the cheerleaders lining up in front of me and chanting ''Down with Claire! Down with Claire!'' I kept glancing at Alan and alternately wishing he would notice me and praying he hadn't. I felt so uncomfortable that I could hardly cheer.

But after a while I got caught up in the spirit of the thing. Jenny was screaming her lungs out and the whole gym was practically electric with energy. When the cheerleaders shouted ''What are we gonna do?'' the crowd yelled back ''Beat Pittsford!'' with such intensity that the walls seemed to shake. How could I not join in?

After a few introductory cheers, Alan gave a little speech, thanking everyone for putting an end to football vandalism. When he was finished the crowd cheered, and Alan looked so pleased he practically glowed. Looking at Alan, I felt happy for him, but I felt a little sad, too, because I knew he wouldn't share his happiness with me. I wasn't a part of his life anymore, and although I knew him well enough to guess what he was feeling, I couldn't talk to him about it. I wasn't his girlfriend anymore.

After Alan's speech, the pep club took the floor for the pom-pom cheers. By this time, I was really into the spirit of things. Jumping up and down in the noisy gym, it was easy to forget that I was dating the P. C. quarterback or that I had only attended one Mill game all year. All that mattered was the here and now, and as the pep club spelled out "Go Sultans!" I was practically overflowing with school spirit.

It wasn't until we sat down and listened to the marching band play another song that I realized I had to go to the ladies' room. Whispering to Jenny, "I'll be right back," I hopped off the bleachers and hurried out the door. The lobby was empty and so was the rest room. In a minute I was hurrying back across the lobby, eager to get back to the gym.

That was when I heard the honking. It sounded like about ten cars, wildly beeping their horns. A wedding? I wondered, but it seemed a little late in the day for that.

Curious, I walked to the doors that led to the parking lot. Cupping my hands around my eyes, I leaned against the door and looked out. In the dim light, I could make out three cars, racing across the parking lot toward the school. As they got closer, I saw that one of the cars was small and blue. Vaguely, I was aware that it looked a lot like Doug's car. As I tried to decide if it was his car, all three cars screeched up to the curb and stopped.

After that, everything seemed to happen at once. The car doors opened and Doug and three of his football buddies jumped out. With cans of spray paint in their hands, they advanced toward the school, whooping and laughing wildly. For a moment I was too horrified to move. I just stood there, staring out the door as Doug began writing RAVENS RULE across the broad cement sidewalk.

Then, suddenly, something inside me seemed to snap. My trust and gullibility seemed to vanish, like leaves in the wind. No longer could I convince myself that what Doug was doing was a joke or a harmless prank. No longer could I tell myself to loosen up and relax. Spray painting graffiti on the sidewalk was nothing less than vandalism. It was illegal and just plain stupid.

Throwing open the door, I stepped onto the sidewalk and shouted, "Doug! Just what do you think you're doing?"

The other boys froze and stared at me, but Doug only grinned. "Hey, Claire, grab a can," he said coolly. "We're gonna leave a little message for the kids inside."

I was so shocked I could barely respond. Did Doug really think I was going to pick up a can of spray paint and help him? Did he actually expect me to deface my own school? "Doug," I shouted, "you must be out of your mind! Get out of here! Now!"

Before Doug could reply, the shrill whine of a siren split the air and in the distance I saw a series of flashing red lights. "The cops!" Doug cried frantically. "Let's go!"

The boys jumped into their cars, but it was too late. Before they'd even pulled away from the curb, two police cars were there, blocking their only path of escape. Simultaneously, I heard shouting behind me and when I turned around I saw Alan and Mr. Bower with two security guards, running across the lobby toward me. Behind them, a few kids were peering curiously around the gymnasium doors.

Mr. Bower and the security guards burst through the doors with Alan close behind. "We heard the sirens," Mr. Bower explained. "What's going on?"

The policemen were out of their cars by now. "Our radar clocked these kids going ninety down Blackrock

Road," one of them said. "We followed them here."

Mr. Bower turned to me. "And what about you? What are you doing out here?"

I looked at Doug. He had gotten out of his car and was standing there staring at me. His eyes, angry and intense, seemed to burn into mine. What was he trying to tell me? I wondered. Did he want me to lie for him? To tell the police it had all been my idea? Or did he expect me to laugh and tell Mr. Bower to "lighten up, it's just a joke"?

Confused, I turned away from Doug and glanced at Alan. He looked worried and uncertain. His eyes seemed to be asking, Is it true? Were you really involved in this?

For a moment, I hesitated. Should I lie for Doug or tell Alan the truth? I looked at Alan one more time. His eyes were pleading. Tell me it isn't true, they seemed to say.

"I was coming from the ladies' room when I heard some car horns," I said quickly. "I looked outside and saw these guys drive up. When they started spray painting the sidewalk, I told them to stop. Then the police showed up."

"She was inside at the pep rally," Alan said. "I'm sure she wasn't involved in this."

He believed me! I was so happy I wanted to grab Alan and hug him, but when I caught his eye and smiled, he looked away.

"Okay, boys," the policeman said. "Let's go down to the station and call your folks."

Doug scowled at me as he got into the police car. Immediately, all my good feeling seemed to vanish. Miserably, I turned away. I had ratted on my boyfriend, and it didn't feel good. Sure, he deserved it, but right now that didn't matter. I had betrayed Doug and I felt like a real rat.

135

By now the word had spread throughout the gym that something was going on outside. Kids were crowding into the lobby to get a look, and at least a dozen people had come outside. I saw Barry Fitch run up to the police cars and take a quick look inside.

"Everybody back in the gym," Mr. Bower ordered.

"What happened?" someone asked.

"Claire Mason's P. C. boyfriend got arrested." It was Barry, of course, eager to spread the bad news.

"P. C. stinks!" Matt Rosselli shouted. He shook his fist at the departing police cars. A few other kids joined in.

"Claire was out there with him," I heard a girl say.

In a matter of seconds, word spread from outside the school to inside the lobby. Everyone knew that "Claire's P. C. boyfriend" had been arrested and that I had been outside when it happened.

"Claire was helping them!" I heard someone shout.

"Inside! Everybody!" Mr. Bower and the security guards were trying to herd the kids back through the doors.

"What's the idea?" Matt asked loudly. "Don't you have any school loyalty?"

I looked at the crowd. Everyone was staring at me. I could feel my face turning red and tears stung the corners of my eyes. "I didn't do anything," I said miserably. "I just—"

I looked around for Alan. He would stick up for me. He would understand. But Alan wasn't in sight. Bitterly, I imagined he had gone inside to find Wendy Hill. Probably he was holding her hand and reassuring her. "Everything is under control," I pictured him saying. "It was just Claire and her stupid boyfriend, trying to show off."

"It wasn't me!" I insisted, but no one even heard me. The security guards had finally persuaded everyone to go inside. The lobby was emptying out as the kids drifted back into the gym.

But I didn't follow. How could I? No one wanted me at the pep rally—not even Alan. I wasn't a part of the Mill anymore. Miserably, I watched as the security guards followed Mr. Bower into the gym and closed the doors.

It was quiet now. The only evidence of what had happened was the half-finished message on the sidewalk: RAVENS RU—. With tears in my eyes, I turned away from the school and headed back to my car. As I drove away I could hear the marching band launch into a spirited rendition of "Miller's Township, Ere We Hail," but to me it sounded as foreign as the Yugoslavian national anthem. The Mill wasn't my school anymore.

Chapter Fourteen

When the alarm rang the next morning, I didn't get up. There was no way I could face going to school today. No way. At seven-thirty Dad stuck his head in and said, "Up and at 'em. You don't want to miss the bus." I grunted a response and Dad went away. Immediately, I rolled over and closed my eyes. I knew if I waited a few more minutes Dad would leave for work and I'd be free to do what I wanted—mainly, crawl in a hole and die.

But I'd forgotten one thing. We get the *Pittsford Herald* delivered to our house each morning and Dad always glances at the headlines on his way out the door. At exactly 8:05 he was back, newspaper in hand.

"Claire," he said firmly. "Wake up." I opened my eyes and found Dad hovering above me, an I-mean-business look on his face. "What do you know about this?" he demanded.

Reluctantly, I sat up and looked at the paper. FOOTBALL

VANDALS ARRESTED, the headline read. FOUR PITTSFORD CEN-
TRAL TEENAGERS CHARGED WITH DEFACING MILLER'S TOWNSHIP
PROPERTY.

"Nothing," I muttered.

"Nothing?" Dad repeated incredulously. "Just listen
to this." He opened the paper and started to read. "When
police arrived, Claire Mason, a Miller's Township student, was standing near the doors outside the school. The
student claimed she had heard a noise and gone outside to
see what was happening. Student council president Alan
Wallant confirmed that she had been at the pep rally
earlier in the evening." Dad looked up from the paper.
"Well?"

"Well what?" I asked defensively.

"I had no idea Doug was the kind of boy who would do
something like this," he said. "Claire, I'm very disappointed in you."

I sat up in bed and stared at my father. "Hey, *I* wasn't
the one who got in trouble. I just heard them out there.
When I saw what was going on, I tried to stop them." My
father didn't say anything and I felt like I was going down
for the third time. Didn't he believe me, either? "Dad," I
pleaded, "I'm telling the truth."

"I don't doubt it, Claire, but I'm still disappointed.
You must have known what kind of boy Doug was, and
yet you still went out with him. Why?"

I looked at my father and felt anger flash through me
like a hot flame. If Dad really cared about me, I told
myself, he would know why I'd gone out with Doug. If he
had any interest in me at all, he would understand how
crummy I'd felt the last few months, how much I missed
Mom, and how sick of Miller's Creek I was. Most of all,

140

he would have realized that I was confused and that I needed him to help me.

But no, I told myself, Dad was too busy with his own life to care about mine. All he wanted to do was get rid of me so he could enjoy Miller's Creek in peace. He would be delighted to see me move to Boston, I was sure. Probably as soon as I moved out, he would start spending every minute with his new girlfriend, Ellen Bresner.

I realize now that most of what I was thinking didn't make much sense. But at the time, I was so angry, and so miserable, it all seemed perfectly reasonable.

"You want to know why I dated Doug?" I cried belligerently. "To get out of Miller's Creek, that's why. To get away from *you!*"

As soon as the words left my mouth, I regretted them. Dad looked like I'd punched him in the stomach and I wanted to throw my arms around him and apologize. But before I could do anything, Dad's face hardened into an expressionless mask. "Get dressed, young lady," he told me. "I'm taking you to school."

As soon as Dad left the room, I got up and threw some clothes on. My mind was a confused jumble of thoughts—all of them bad. I knew Dad was outside waiting for me in the truck and I knew I should go down and apologize. But something inside me said no. I hadn't done anything wrong. If anyone should apologize, I told myself, it was Dad.

The other thing that was worrying me was school. How could I go back there and face the kids? Most of them probably thought I'd been out there with Doug last night, helping him paint RAVENS RULE on the sidewalk. Even if some of them believed me, they undoubtedly thought I was a moron for ever dating Doug in the first place. And what about Alan? How did he feel? All I knew was that last night when I really needed him, he had turned away. I think that was what hurt the most.

Dad honked the horn and I knew if I didn't go downstairs, he'd come up and get me. Reluctantly, I ran a brush through my hair and hurried downstairs. Okay, I told myself, so Dad was going to drive me to school. So what? That still didn't mean I had to go inside. I'd just wait until he drove off and then leave.

On the way to school, neither Dad nor I said anything. I don't know what he was thinking, but my mind was filled with crazy schemes. I would run away, I told myself. I would hitchhike to New York City. But no, angry as I was, I knew that was a bad idea—too dangerous, too scary. Okay, then, I'd catch a bus to Boston. But all I had in my pocket was twelve dollars, barely enough to get me halfway there. Well, at least I could call Mom. She'd understand. When she learned how unhappy I was, she'd probably catch the first bus out here and get me.

When Dad pulled up in front of the school, I got out and walked slowly toward the front door. But as soon as he drove away, I turned around and ran to the side of the building. Homeroom had already started, so no one was around. With a determined stride, I started off across the field, toward the Mini Mart on Brookside Road.

There's a pay phone outside the Mini Mart and I headed straight for it. Keeping an eye out for Dad's truck, I put in a dime and placed a collect call to Mom. A male voice answered, ''Hello?'' It was one of Mom's housemates.

''Collect call from Claire,'' the operator said. ''Will you accept the charges?''

"Uh, sure," the voice said. "I guess so. Is this Claire Mason? Marie's daughter?"

"Yes," I answered. "Is my mom there?"

"Sorry, Claire. She left about twenty minutes ago. Do you want her number at work?"

"Okay." I got the number, put in another dime, and called the restaurant where Mom works, but whoever answered wouldn't accept a collect call. The only thing to do was to get some change. I went into the Mini Mart, bought a package of cookies, and asked for two dollars in quarters.

Back at the phone, I called again and found out I had to pay $2.05 for three minutes. Well, what could I do? I put my money in the slot and watched it disappear.

"The Vegetarian Venture," a female voice said.

"Is Marie Mason there?" I asked.

"Sorry. We're not even open yet. No one's here but me. But let me check the schedule." I heard papers rustling. "She's not in till eleven today. Can I take a message?"

I was so disappointed it was all I could do to answer. "Just tell her that her daughter called," I said. "That's all."

As soon as I hung up, I started to cry. It was silly, I guess, but I couldn't help it. It just felt so rotten and so alone. Mom was probably out studying in a library somewhere and I wouldn't be able to talk to her for at least two and a half hours. I almost felt like talking to Dad, but I was still mad, and besides, what would I say? He'd probably just yell at me for skipping school and then I'd say something stupid and things would be worse than ever.

Miserably, I sat down next to the phone booth and ate

the entire bag of cookies. When I was finished I felt sick, but I didn't care. At this point, I didn't even care if Dad drove by and saw me or if a truant officer came along and picked me up. I didn't care about anything at all.

That's when I remembered Mrs. Rosemont. Maybe—just maybe—I could talk to her. True, I didn't know her very well, but during that one afternoon we'd spent together, we'd really hit it off. Besides, Mrs. Rosemont was an amazing lady. She'd lived in Miller's Creek and she'd traveled all over the world. She obviously knew a lot about life. Maybe I was just grasping at straws, but I had a feeling she'd be a good person to talk to. Anyhow, Dad had told me Mrs. Rosemont would probably like to see me again and today was as good a time as any.

Valley View Nursing Home was probably two miles away from the Mill, but I didn't care. I started down the road at a brisk pace. Now that I had somewhere to go, I felt better. It was a cold day, but I walked quickly, shuffling my feet through the fallen leaves as I went. Some of the trees were bare but others still glowed with color. By concentrating on the scenery I was able to block out all the rotten things that were going on in my life, and by the time I got to Valley View I actually felt pretty good.

In the lobby, I told the receptionist I wanted to see Mrs. Rosemont. She dialed a number, muttered a few words into the telephone, and then told me to go up to her room. "Just take the elevator to the third floor," she explained. "Room three thirty-two."

The third-floor hallway looked like the hallway in a fancy apartment building. There was plush carpeting on the floor and framed prints on the wall. I found room 332 and knocked.

"Come in, Claire," Mrs. Rosemont called.

I walked in and found Mrs. Rosemont sitting in her wheelchair in the middle of an attractive, cluttered living room. There were books and papers piled on the tables and framed photographs all over the walls. Mrs. Rosemont looked almost the same as the last time I had seen her. Her white hair was a little longer and she had on a wool skirt and sweater instead of jeans, but her bright-blue eyes were as lively as I'd remembered them and her face was just as kind.

"Hello," Mrs. Rosemont said cheerfully. "It's wonderful to see you again. Sit down."

I took a seat on the sofa and smiled uncertainly. Now that I was there, I wasn't sure what to say. How could I just dump my problems on this nice old lady? I barely knew her.

But Mrs. Rosemont was leaning forward in her wheelchair, looking at me expectantly. She didn't seem the least bit surprised to see me. In fact, I got the feeling she was just waiting for me to get started. I took a deep breath, opened my mouth, and immediately began to cry.

Instantly, Mrs. Rosemont wheeled herself over and patted my knee. "Poor Claire," she said softly. "It's been a tough time for you, hasn't it? It's been difficult for Alan, too."

"W-what?" I felt like I'd been thrown into the middle of a surrealist play or something. I knew all the characters, but I couldn't make sense of the plot. "What do you mean?" I asked, sniffing loudly.

"Since that afternoon you two interviewed me, Alan has stopped by almost every week." Mrs. Rosemont smiled. "He really cares about you, Claire."

"Oh, sure," I said sarcastically. It was hard enough to believe Alan had even mentioned me, let alone said something nice.

"I mean it. We talk about you a lot. He was very upset when you started going out with that boy from Pittsford."

"Then why did he let me?" I asked bitterly. "Why didn't he just tell me to drop Doug and come back to him?"

Mrs. Rosemont smiled. "Alan's not that kind of boy, Claire. He has too much respect for you to tell you what to do. Besides, you hurt him. Maybe he felt he had to hurt you a little, too."

I sighed deeply. "I guess I deserved it. But Mrs. Rosemont, Doug was hard to resist. I mean, he's so handsome and exciting. And he comes from Pittsford. When he asked me out, I figured it was a way to get out of Miller's Creek for a while." I was talking even faster than usual now, trying to explain. "This town is so boring," I said. "You must know what I mean. You've been all over the world."

"Of course I do." Mrs. Rosemont handed me a tissue and waited while I blew my nose. "Some people just weren't meant to live in a small town. They need the excitement of the city to make them happy."

I nodded enthusiastically. "That's me all right."

"But if I learned one thing from my travels, Claire, it's this: Every place has something to offer. No matter how small, each town has something special, something that makes it unique."

As I listened to Mrs. Rosemont I thought about all the years I'd lived in Miller's Creek. I remembered the wonderful afternoons I had spent in the treehouse that my father had built, and the fun I'd had catching tadpoles in the creek. I thought about how much I loved our old stone farmhouse and how beautiful it looked ablaze with Christmas lights.

Why, even in the past few months, I'd had some good times in Miller's Creek. I remembered sitting in the McClintocks' kitchen, eating eggs and bacon and laughing with my father and the other firemen. Walking home from school with Alan, reminiscing with Dad, cheering at the pep rally—they had all been special times. And they had all taken place in Miller's Creek.

"You're right," I said, smiling feebly. Sighing, I added, "You know, I thought going out with Doug would be different. I figured he'd take me to special places and show me things I couldn't see in Miller's Creek." I laughed ruefully. "But it was just the same. All we did was go to football games and eat at fast-food restaurants. The only time it was really exciting was when Doug did something illegal—and even then it was more frightening than fun."

Mrs. Rosemont smiled knowingly. "That's another thing I've learned over the years. It's not the place that counts—it's the people. That's not to say that China is no different from Miller's Creek. It most certainly is! But there are good people and bad people, boring people and vital people everywhere. You just have to look around until you find them."

Looking into Mrs. Rosemont's clear blue eyes, I had to admit she was right. Two months ago I never would have believed that anyone as amazing as Mrs. Rosemont could be found in the Valley View Nursing Home. And yet here she was. All I'd had to do was look for her.

And come to think of it, my father was another example. Until the night he'd told me about his cross-country trip, I'd just assumed his life had been uneventful and dull. Who would have ever guessed Dad was the type to just take off across the country in a battered old 1951 Chevy? But he had. He actually had!

With a sinking feeling, I remembered how rude I'd been to my father this morning. Would he ever forgive me? I wondered. And what about Alan? At this point, I didn't expect him to want me back, but maybe we could still be friends. If he'd just give me another chance . . .

Mrs. Rosemont's gentle laughter brought me back from my thoughts. "Don't look so forlorn, Claire," she told me. "Things will work out. A few kind words at the right moment can do wonders. Just wait and see."

I smiled gratefully. "Mrs. Rosemont," I said, "I sure hope you're right."

Chapter Fifteen

When I finally left Mrs. Rosemont, it was almost three o'clock. On the long walk home, I thought about all the things we'd talked about. I even figured out a couple for myself.

I guess the most important thing I figured out is this: Life is not a magazine quiz. That sounds pretty obvious, I know, but what I mean is, the world is really complicated. You can't just ask yourself a lot of simplistic questions like "Which do you like better—the city or the country?" and then plan your whole life based on the answers.

For example, just because I don't like every single thing about Miller's Creek doesn't mean I have to reject it completely. Like Mrs. Rosemont said, every town, no matter how small, has something to offer. Sure, Miller's Creek can get pretty dull sometimes, and I know I wouldn't want to live here forever. But as long as I'm here now, I might as well try to enjoy myself, right?

Another thing that isn't simple is people. You can't just ask someone what flavor ice cream he likes and then think you've got him all figured out. Take Doug, for example. Just because he's handsome and he comes from Pittsford, I thought he was really hot stuff. But when you come right down to it, Doug isn't so wonderful. All he knows how to do is drive fast, talk tough, and show off. What's so special about that?

And then there's Alan. I thought I was too sophisticated for a country boy like him. But when you think about it, Alan is no hick. He's intelligent, he's sensitive, and he can be just as tough as Doug when he wants to be. Like that time he stood up to Barry Fitch and Matt Rosselli in the cafeteria. That took a lot more guts than Doug would ever have, and a lot more good sense, too.

When I finally got home and unlocked the front door, the phone was ringing. Reluctantly, I picked it up, expecting to hear my father screaming, "Why weren't you in school today?"

Instead, it was my mother. "Claire," she said urgently, "I got your message. Is everything all right?"

I had to laugh. So much had happened since this morning, I'd completely forgotten that I'd left a message for my mother to call back. "Well," I told her, "things aren't exactly great, but they're a heck of a lot better than they were."

"Honey, I'm at work and I can't talk long. Please tell me what's wrong."

"I had a fight with Dad," I said. "But we'll work it

out. I'm sorry I bothered you. Really.''

"Claire, you could never be a bother. You're my daughter and I love you.''

"I love you, too, Mom.''

There was a lot of noise on Mom's end of the line and I heard someone say, ''Marie, hang up and get table three.''

"I've got to go, Claire,'' she said. ''But I'll call you tonight. And remember, we'll see each other at Thanksgiving. Then we can really talk.''

"Okay, Mom. Don't work too hard. Good-bye.''

After I hung up, I walked around the house, searching for something to do. I felt lost and distracted and I guess I was worried about facing Dad when he came home from work. Then suddenly I had an idea. The night Dad and I had stayed up reminiscing, he'd told me that my old treehouse was still standing. Maybe I'd go out back and find it. If it wasn't falling apart, I could even climb up and take a look around.

Throwing on a jacket, I ran out into the backyard. We have almost two acres of land around our house, and the section near the back is almost all trees. Eagerly, I followed my old method for finding the correct tree—go through the apples trees, turn right at the rosebush, then count four trees from the old stump. I looked up and there it was, nestled in the crook of the red maple tree!

I grabbed for the lowest branch and pulled myself up. The treehouse was old and weathered, but only a couple of the boards looked rotten. Gingerly, I climbed up and stepped into the treehouse. There were bird droppings and acorn shells all over the floor, but I didn't care. It was still

my secret castle and the backyard was my magic kingdom. Happily, I sat down and inhaled the fresh scent of
leaves, dirt, and bark.

"Claire? Are you up there?"

When I heard my father's voice, I was so surprised I
practically fell out of the tree. How long had I been up
here? I wondered. Was it dinnertime already? And how
had Dad known I was here?

I stuck my head out and looked down. Dad was leaning
against the trunk of the tree, looking up. I smiled uncertainly. "Hi. I'll be right down."

"Don't bother," Dad replied. "I'll come up." Before I
could answer Dad grabbed the bottom branch and heaved
himself up into the tree. "Not bad for an old fellow," he
said, gasping for breath.

I giggled as he climbed up and peered into the
treehouse. "Are you sure it will hold us both?" I asked.

Dad patted the boards. "I built this to last," he said, but
I noticed he sat down gently and kept his arm hooked
around the nearest branch.

"How did you know I'd be here?" I asked.

"Just a hunch. Look, Claire, about this morning—"

"Dad, I'm sorry. I didn't mean to be so obnoxious. I
was just upset about the pep rally, I guess."

"You've been upset about a lot of things lately and I
don't blame you. All this divorce stuff has been harder on
you than on anyone, I think. It's not easy to understand
why your mom and I are happier apart than together." He
sighed. "I don't really understand it myself."

"Yeah, well, I guess Mom just wasn't meant to live in

the country and be a housewife. It's just not her style."

Dad nodded. "Not yours, either, I suppose. That's why I want you to finish the year in Boston with your mother. I know it's what you want, too."

That was when I realized I absolutely did *not* want to finish my senior year in Boston. I don't know what made me so certain. Maybe it had something to do with the talk I'd had with Mrs. Rosemont. Or maybe it was walking home through Miller's Creek and realizing I kind of like it here. Then again, maybe it was knowing I had a father who liked climbing trees and who could put up with a daughter like me. Whatever the reason, I knew for certain I wanted to stay in Miller's Creek with Dad.

"Forget it, Dad." My father looked up in surprise. "Just forget it," I repeated. "I'm not leaving."

"You want to stay here?" he asked doubtfully.

"Yeah, sure. Listen, I'll be going to college in Boston next year, anyway. Besides . . ." I looked down at my hands. For some reason, I felt suddenly shy. "Besides, Dad, I want to be with you. I know I've been kind of a jerk lately, but . . ." I looked into my father's face. "Daddy, I love you."

Dad held out his arms and we hugged each other tightly. "I love you, too, Claire," he said softly. As we moved apart, the boards beneath us creaked ominously. "I guess this treehouse wasn't designed for two," Dad told me. "We'd better climb down."

Dad went first and I followed. As we walked slowly toward the house he said, "Now listen, Claire. If you're going to stay here—and believe me, I want you to—you have to promise me one thing. No more lies. And no more locking yourself in the bathroom. If you're upset about something, let's talk it over. And no more jumping to conclusions, either. For example, I am *not* dating Ellen Bresner. Understand?''

''That's more than one thing, Dad.'' I giggled. ''That's about twelve.''

''Never mind, smarty-pants. And another thing. If you want to think I'm a hopelessly boring country bumpkin, that's your prerogative. But don't rub it in, okay?''

''Oh, Daddy! I'm sorry. I don't think you're boring. Really. I was just mad.''

''Did I ever tell you about the time I took a tramp steamer to Mexico?''

''No,'' I said, my voice full of awe. ''Tell me about it.''

Dad put his arm around my shoulders and gave me a squeeze. ''Later,'' he said. ''First I want to hear about what's been going on with you. I feel like we've been completely out of touch lately. I'll make dinner and you tell me what's been happening. What do you say?''

''It's a deal,'' I said, following him into the house.

During dinner, I told Dad all about my troubles at the Mill. ''They all hate me,'' I said. ''How can I ever go back?''

''It won't be easy,'' Dad said sympathetically. ''But if you're going to finish your senior year in Miller's Creek, there's no way to avoid it.'' He looked thoughtful. ''Tomorrow is Homecoming, right?''

I frowned. ''Yeah, I guess so. I was trying to forget.''

''Well, why don't you go?'' I groaned loudly, but Dad

kept talking. "You want to get back in the swing of things, right?" I nodded. "Well, what better way is there? Go to the game and cheer for the Mill as loud as you can. Show everyone you still care."

"Well, maybe," I said doubtfully. "But I'm sure to get hassled."

"I know. But it can't go on forever. After a while everyone will get tired of teasing you." Dad patted my shoulder and smiled. "I know it's not easy, hon. Kids in little towns can be awfully small-minded. But things will get better. You'll see."

In bed that night, I thought over my father's suggestion. Maybe he was right, I decided. Maybe I should go to the Homecoming game. After all, I went to the pep rally and that hadn't been too bad—until Doug and his crazy friends had shown up, of course.

Well, I reminded myself, at least I wouldn't have to worry about Doug interfering with Homecoming. During the football game, he'd be too busy playing to get into trouble. And according to the evening paper, the cops had ordered him and his pals to spend the rest of the afternoon cleaning the graffiti off the sidewalk.

But then I thought of Alan. What if I went to the Homecoming game and saw him with Wendy Hill? I'd just die. On the other hand, maybe he'd be alone and I'd be able to talk to him. Maybe I could even get up the nerve to apologize. The worst he could do was tell me to drop dead, and after all, that's about what I deserved.

Feeling both determined and frightened, I made up my mind. I would go to Homecoming tomorrow.

*　　*　　*

The next day I was just getting ready to leave for the game when the telephone rang. Dropping my car keys on the kitchen counter, I lifted the receiver. "Hello?"

"Hey, Claire, what's happening?"

When I heard Doug's voice, I gasped. Pretty melodramatic, I know, but I was really shocked. After what had happened at the pep rally, I never expected to hear from Doug again. And to tell you the truth, I didn't want to. "Doug," I managed to say, "what do you want?"

"Just wanted to tell you when I'm picking you up tonight. I'll be over around seven-thirty."

My mind was reeling. Was this some kind of joke? "Pick me up?" I repeated blankly. "For what?"

"The Victory Bash," he said coolly. "We've got a date, you know."

I couldn't believe it. Did Doug really think I still wanted to go out with him? What conceit! "Sorry, Doug," I said, "but I'm not going. I don't date guys whose idea of a good time is breaking the law. I might have once, but I wised up."

Now it was Doug's turn to be shocked. "But if you don't come with me, who will I take? You don't expect me to go to this dance alone, do you?" When I didn't answer, he tried to turn on the charm. "Hey, Claire," he said softly, "I thought we really had something together. Remember that afternoon we drove down the fire road?"

In the past, Doug's sexy voice had made my knees weak, but now I felt nothing at all. And when I remembered the fire road, all I thought about was Alan and the wonderful times we'd had together there. "Sorry, Doug. I'm not interested."

"Oh, yeah? Well, don't think you're the only girl I go out with, Mason. I don't need to date someone from the Mill, anyway. That school is strictly a dump. I know—"

"Listen, Doug," I said firmly, "there's only one thing you need to know and it's this: I'm not going out with you tonight, tomorrow, or ever again. Understand?"

I didn't hear Doug's answer because I hung up the phone. Then I grabbed my keys and hurried out of the house.

The parking lot was almost full when I pulled in next to the Miller's Township stadium. It was an Indian summer day—unseasonably warm and sunny—and everybody had shown up early to work on their tans. I got out of the car, took a deep breath, and headed for the bleachers. Last night I had decided to come to the game alone, but now I almost wished I had called Jenny. I could have used a little moral support.

Inside the stadium, things were already happening. The visitor stands and the home bleachers were both filled to the brim with noisy, enthusiastic football fans. The marching band was blasting away and the Homecoming parade was in full swing. The bleachers were so full I just stood near the bottom row and watched as the student council float came by. The float was built on the back of a flatbed truck and Alan, I noticed, was the driver. Two kids rode on the back of the truck—one dressed as a sultan, the other as a raven. A sign on the side of the truck read "PITTSFORD CENTRAL AND MILLER'S TOWNSHIP: FRIENDSHIP, FAIR PLAY, AND TRUST."

If this were last year, I reflected sadly, I would be in that parade, not watching from the sidelines. As I watched Alan go by, I longed to be sitting next to him. He was proud of that float, I was sure, and I wished I could share it with him. But how could I? I was probably the last person in the world Alan would want on a float that represented friendship, fair play, and trust. As far as he was concerned, I was part of the reason things were so tense between P. C. and the Mill this year.

After the parade, I walked into the bleachers and managed to find a seat about halfway up. Naturally, I didn't go unnoticed. Heads turned, I heard whispers behind my back, and a couple of boys asked, "Why don't you go over to the P. C. side where you belong?"

But I kept thinking about what Dad had told me last night. "Kids in little towns can be awfully small-minded," he'd said. "But things will get better." Boy, I hoped he was right. I ignored the stares, and when the cheerleaders came out I jumped up and joined in the cheers with all the enthusiasm I could muster.

Later, when the P. C. team came on the field, I looked for Doug. There he was—number 33—strong and sleek in his red-and-white uniform. Over the last two months I had wasted a lot of time and energy cheering and applauding his every move. But no more. As I looked at Doug now, I felt nothing. Absolutely nothing. I didn't have the slightest urge to cheer.

Then the Miller's Township team ran onto the field, and like everyone else I was on my feet and screaming. When the cheerleaders asked, "What are we gonna do?" I raised my fist and yelled, "Beat Pittsford!"

It was at that moment that I spotted Alan. He was

walking up the steps between the rows of bleachers and he was heading right for me. Well, he was heading in my general direction. I couldn't tell if he'd seen me or not because he was looking down at his feet.

This is your big chance, I told myself. Talk to him, Claire. Say his name. My heart was pounding in my ears and my hands were sweating. What if he wouldn't talk to me? What if he ignored me? But no, he wouldn't do that. Mrs. Rosemont had said that Alan still cared about me. She'd said he'd talked about me a lot.

All right, Mason, I told myself firmly. Here he comes. Talk to him. Now. "Alan?" I managed to bleat.

Alan stopped and looked at me. I tried to read his expression, but I couldn't. Mostly he just looked shocked.

"Uh, hi," I said lamely.

"Hi, Claire." He smiled slightly and my heart leaped with joy. "How are you?"

I giggled foolishly. "Uh, pretty lousy, to tell you the truth."

Alan looked like he wasn't sure what to do next. "Oh?" he said finally.

"Yeah, well, I . . . uh . . . really want to talk to you, and, uh, you know, apologize." Alan didn't say anything so I stumbled on. "But, well, I don't really know how to start and, uh, you'll probably just tell me to get lost and, uh, well, to tell you the truth, I feel like a first-class jerk." I gulped and rubbed my sweaty palms against my jeans. Down on the field the game had begun, and around us the crowd was clapping and cheering. But all I could think of was Alan. I looked into his face. His blond hair was being tousled by the breeze and I could see my reflection in his soulful gray eyes. What is he thinking? I wondered miserably.

Then, slowly, the corners of Alan's mouth lifted into a smile. My spirits soared as he reached out and took my hand. "Come on," he said. "Let's go somewhere where we can talk."

Alan led me down the stairs and across the front of the bleachers. Still holding his hand, I followed him around the corner, past the refreshment stand, and finally underneath the bleachers. No one was around except a couple of little kids who were giggling and tossing a miniature football back and forth.

Alan dropped my hand and looked at me shyly. "Well . . ." he began, and then stopped.

"Well . . ." I agreed and we both laughed foolishly. I took a deep breath and started again. "Look, Alan, you told me once you wanted me back, but only if I wanted you, too. Well, I do. I really do." I hesitated. "That is, if you haven't changed your mind."

Alan's face was filled with pain. "These last couple of months have been really tough on me, Claire. As student council president, I've had to defend your right to date anyone you choose. And I believe that, too. I mean, P. C., the Mill—it's really all the same. But inside I was just as mad as Barry Fitch or Matt Rosselli or anybody. All I wanted to do was bust Doug Landsberg's nose." He looked at me angrily and then stopped himself and smiled. "Hey, who am I trying to kid? I want you back, Claire. I have all along. Even when I was really mad at you, I still hoped you'd come back."

When I heard that, I threw my arms around Alan and

hugged him for all I was worth. "Oh, Alan," I said softly, "I love you. I really do."

Alan leaned close and whispered, "I love you, too." Then he kissed me and I felt as if I'd finally come home. Everything around us seemed to disappear. The noisy crowd of people cheering above us, the little kids tossing the football around, the people buying hot dogs at the refreshment stand nearby—nothing mattered except Alan and me and the love we shared.

When the kiss ended, Alan drew back and smiled at me. "I've missed you, Claire."

"I've missed you, too. And boy, I have a lot to tell you. About my parents and about Mrs. Rosemont. And the pep rally. I really was innocent, Alan. You know, I—"

Alan put his hand over my lips. "Tell me tonight," he said. "We'll have plenty of time at the Homecoming dance."

"But Alan," I exclaimed, "I thought you were taking Wendy Hill!"

He frowned. "No way. That was a one-date relationship. Believe me, she's not my type."

"Oh, yeah?" I smiled. "And who is your type, Mr. President?"

Alan grinned and kissed my nose. "Y." Another kiss. "O." One more, this time on the lips. "U!" He kissed me again. "Now let's get out of here. We're missing the big game."

Alan took my hand and together we walked back to the bleachers. Heads turned, kids nudged each other and pointed, but I didn't care. I didn't feel like an outcast anymore. The Mill was my school and Alan was my boyfriend. For the first time in months, I knew I was where I belonged.

When a teen looks for romance, she's looking for

_____	**BEFORE LOVE**	16846-4/ $1.95
_____	**THE BOY NEXT DOOR**	07186-4/ $2.25
_____	**A BICYCLE BUILT FOR TWO**	05733-0/ $1.95
_____	**CARRIE LOVES SUPERMAN**	09178-4/ $1.95
_____	**DANCE WITH A STRANGER**	13609-5/ $1.95
_____	**DO YOU REALLY LOVE ME?**	16053-0/ $1.95
_____	**A HAT FULL OF LOVE**	31787-1/ $1.95
_____	**HEARTBREAKER**	31973-4/ $1.95
_____	**HEARTWAVES**	31991-2/ $1.95
_____	**THE HIDDEN HEART**	32908-X/ $1.95
_____	**LAST KISS IN APRIL**	47119-6/ $1.95
_____	**LOVE BYTE**	49543-5/ $1.95
_____	**LOVE IN FOCUS**	49630-X/ $1.95
_____	**LOVE NOTES**	49703-9/ $2.25
_____	**A NEW FACE IN THE MIRROR**	57123-9/ $2.25

Prices may be slightly higher in Canada.

Available at your local bookstore or return this form to:

TEMPO
Book Mailing Service
P.O. Box 690, Rockville Centre, NY 11571

Please send me the titles checked above. I enclose _____. Include 75¢ for postage and handling if one book is ordered; 25¢ per book for two or more not to exceed $1.75. California, Illinois, New York and Tennessee residents please add sales tax.

NAME_____

ADDRESS_____

CITY_____STATE/ZIP_____

(allow six weeks for delivery)   T-10

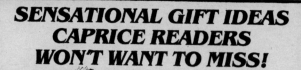
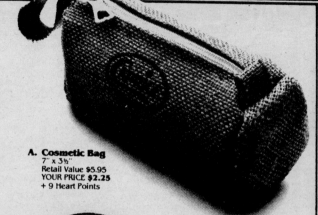

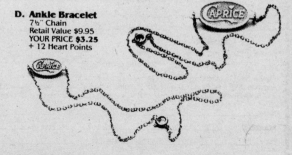

Now that you're reading the best in teen romance, why not make that *Caprice* feeling part of your own special look? Four great gifts to accent that "unique something" in you are all yours when you collect the proof-of-purchase from the back of any current *Caprice* romance!

Each proof-of-purchase is worth 3 Heart Points toward these items available <u>only</u> from *Caprice*. And what better way to make them yours than by reading the romances every teen is talking about! Start collecting today!

Proof-of-purchase is worth 3 Heart Points toward one of four exciting premiums bearing the distinctive *Caprice* logo

CAPRICE PREMIUMS
Berkley Publishing Group, Inc./Dept. LB
200 Madison Avenue, New York, NY 10016

PROOF OF
PURCHASE
—3—
HEART POINTS
♥♥♥
DETAILS INSIDE

SEND ME THESE FABULOUS *CAPRICE* GIFTS:

Quantity	Item and Individual Price	Amount Due
A. _____	**Cosmetic Bag(s)** @ $2.25 + 9 Heart Points each	_____
B. _____	**Key Ring(s)** @ $.75 + 6 Heart Points each	_____
C. _____	**Choker(s)** @ $3.25 + 12 Heart Points each	_____
D. _____	**Ankle Bracelet(s)** @ $3.25 + 12 Heart Points each	_____

Postage and Handling Charge _____
(add $.75 for each item ordered, $1.50 maximum charge)
Total Due $ _____

I have enclosed a check or money order for $_____ (which includes postage and handling charge) with the necessary Heart Points for the *Caprice* premiums indicated above.

NAME_____

ADDRESS_____

CITY_____STATE_____ZIP_____

Allow 4–6 weeks for delivery. Offer good as long as supply lasts. Void where prohibited by law. All state and local regulations apply.

Residents of New York State add appropriate sales tax.

T–11